Prai

BLUE-EYED SLAVE

"*Blue-Eyed Slave* is historically grounded in the racial-equity choices of its time. It is anchored in meticulous research about the details of Jewish life in pre-Civil War Charleston, South Carolina; about a true-life school dedicated to the education of slaves and its profound dangers; and about the moral stances in every generation. The path of a young Jewish girl crosses with the brutal trajectory of a blue-eyed slave girl for sale at the Charleston wharves, and with the life-and-death spectrum of Jewish responses, from cruel conformity to the call to 'tzedakah' (justice). It is a combination of a suspenseful thriller with Talmudic commentary: fasten your seatbelt."

—Jean Riesman PhD

"*Blue-Eyed Slave* is simultaneously a rousing coming-of-age story and a powerful moral tale about the impossible choices ordinary people must sometimes face. What happens to the main characters affects the reader profoundly, so that the horrors of slavery are not simply acknowledged but experienced almost intimately. This historical narrative is that rare thing: a page-turner that enables us to focus more clearly on some of the most painful aspects of the human condition."

—Bruce Bennett
Wells College

"*Blue-Eyed Slave* transported me back in time to what I imagine it might have been like to be a preteen girl growing up in the small, tightly knit Sephardic Jewish community of Charles Town. Marshall Highet and Bird Jones created a world I got lost in for a time. Hannah and her mother, Rebekah, fiercely believe in the Jewish tradition of tzedek—'justice.' This is a lesson we dearly need to remember today. Our country is still dealing with the fact that one group of people owned another. Until we honestly deal with our past and how it still shapes our present, we will never be able to move forward. *Blue-*

Eyed Slave will help families and schools have conversations about how chattel slavery shaped and continues to shape our lives, and these conversations can help us to heal."

—Randi Serrins, MS
Bank Street College of Education, Chair, Historic Coming Street Cemetery Trust

"*Blue-Eyed Slave* is a compelling story of friendship and justice in eighteenth-century Charleston. The reader learns about the life of a Jewish family of merchants who must make difficult decisions when their teenaged daughter, Hannah, befriends a young slave at the slave school where she helps with lessons. The authors have given us detailed history about life in the pre-Revolutionary South as well as strong, independent characters. The Charleston geography and historical context are finely drawn with elements of suspense. A captivating novel!"

—Kate Grannis
Author of the Caerthwaite Series

"*Blue-Eyed Slave* hooked me right away. This is a unique coming-of-age tale of two very different teens whose lives intertwine in Charles Town in 1764. The intricacies of the relationship between a Jewish girl and an African slave girl are at the core of this historically accurate work. Little-known historical facts provide enlightening additions to the story.

"The plot unfolds as Hannah's determination to free Bintu physically and psychologically from a brutal mistress puts her family at risk. Hannah's mother has shielded her from the complexities of slavery, which places her at a disadvantage when she naively goes against the traditions of colonial slavery in order to aid Bintu. Hannah helps the slave girl despite warnings from her family and questions them about living out the acts of justice that are a part of her religious community's spiritual teachings.

"Through trickery and outright opposition to those seeking

to harm Bintu, Hannah and her family devise a dangerous plan designed to save Bintu from certain death. This compelling page-turner is one that readers of all ages will enjoy."

—P. J. McGhee

BLUE-EYED SLAVE

MARSHALL HIGHET
BIRD JONES

VIRGINIA BEACH
CAPE CHARLES

Blue-Eyed Slave

By Marshall Highet and Bird Jones

ISBN 978-1-64663-595-5

Published by

köehlerbooks ™

3705 Shore Drive
Virginia Beach, VA 23455
800–435–4811
www.koehlerbooks.com

June 20, 2021

Dear Reader,

Welcome to the world of Charles Town, South Carolina, 1764, and to Harry's school. Even though this is a work of fiction, Harry was a real person with extraordinary accomplishments. He was a slave, purchased at a young age to teach slave children how to read despite laws forbidding it. What ultimately happened to him is lost to history, but we have attempted to reconstruct who he might have been and how his school would have operated.

Most of the other characters are fictional. If the wicked ones remind you of someone you know, that is pure coincidence. The same is true of the brave or good characters. If our characters come across as living, breathing people, as we hope they do, that is due partly to the historical details we have applied to create them.

What we can tell you for sure is that we paid close attention to minute details and did our best to weave a tale of probability, universal questions, and hope.

Thanks for spending time with us,
Marshall and Bird

MH: For David, always in my corner.

BSJ: For Annie—a voice for justice, a friend for the journey.

CHAPTER 1
1831 Charleston, South Carolina

Looking out the window at the rainy, bleak garden in the dim, winter dusk, I shivered despite the fire at my back.

I'll be eighty this May. Can you imagine? I mused. It seemed like not too long ago I was just a girl, and then the Revolution, and amidst all that, I became a wife, a mother, and an abolitionist. Or despite all that.

My thoughts trailed off as they tended to do more and more. I spent so much time in the past that it was difficult for me to stay in the present.

I tucked some grey curls escaping my cap back into the gingham fabric and turned back to my task of setting the acorn-colored table, smooth from years of polish and good use. Moving creakily and slowly around its long length, I spread the tablecloth and evened its edges. I remembered when my mother, Rebekah, had bought this tablecloth for herself at her own store. It had come in with a shipment of items, and once she had laid eyes on it, that was that.

She had used it for every Shabbat dinner from then on, as I would when it came to be mine.

Friday Shabbat dinner was always a favorite, and I was glad I still felt well enough as an octogenarian to at least do that. I took out a few more candles, readying to light them before sunset. I knew the light would fail soon, darkness would come, and with it, the Sabbath—our day of rest. January Sabbaths were always the darkest.

The table looks lovely, I thought, noting the silver glint of the kiddish cup among the candles. Yes, I was glad I could still do this and wasn't too tired to keep up with family tradition.

The sound of someone singing and the staccato of heels floated down from the floor above me. *Rachel.* Her feet on the stairs sounded like a wooden waterfall. She burst into the room, lighting up the place.

"Nonna, Nonna, I've found something," Rachel sang as she bounded over to where I was lowering myself into a seat at the head of the table for a quick rest. When she reached me, Rachel did a little jig, curls bouncing, still singing, *"I've found such treasures, tra la la."*

This performance, a regular one, evoked a smile as I wondered for the millionth time, *Where, oh where, did you come from, little hummingbird?* As if I didn't recognize my own daughter reimagined.

Rachel's wild hair was more unruly than she, the color of autumn leaves, a cross between burnished gold and auburn with strands of sunlight. Those ridiculous curls bobbed with every twirl and step, framing Rachel's heart-shaped face. I knew from personal experience that those weren't the kind of curls to be tamed.

"Rachel, what am I to do with you?" I teased. "I need you in the kitchen with me, helping with the challah, not off finding treasure." I touched the tip of her nose.

"But look, Nonna, look at what I found!" Rachel thrust her hand into the front pocket of her apron and fished out a thin leather cord with a dangling charm. A necklace. That charm. A *hamsa*—the universal hand of protection for many religions.

I inhaled deeply and closed my eyes. Seeing the necklace again brought all of it back to me so suddenly; it was as if Bintu's ghost walked into the room, bringing a gust of winter air with her. I shivered.

"Nonna?" Rachel asked in alarm.

I exhaled and tried to recover, not wanting to scare the child.

"Did I . . . did I do something wrong, Nonna?"

I shook my head. "No, hummingbird, you did nothing wrong. It's just that . . . it's just that I haven't seen this necklace for a very long time. And it brought back some memories."

"Sad ones?"

"Sad and happy, like all the best ones. Where did you find it, Rachel?"

"In a box, in the back of your trunk in the attic." Rachel, still unconvinced that she wasn't being reprimanded, rubbed at her eyes. "Next to some old medals and stuff."

"And was there anything else with it, Rachel?"

Rachel raised her gaze to mine, her impending tears making them glow a translucent gray, and nodded. From her apron pocket she fished out a scrap of thick paper with the Star of David printed on the front, another sign of protection, not that it had helped Bintu in the end. Or maybe it had, but I would never know.

I took the scrap of paper and unfolded it, reading the Hebrew words out loud:

Tzedek Tzedek Tirdof
Justice, justice shall you pursue that you may live,
and inherit the land which the Lord your God gives you
Bintu

Rachel was holding up the necklace, admiring the silver charm as it caught the firelight. "Who gave you this, Nonna? Was it a friend of yours?"

I reached out to take the hand-shaped charm into my own wrinkled one. "Yes, she was. My very best friend. Would you like to hear about her?"

"Would I!" Rachel plunked herself on a wooden footstool in front of me, her stick-like legs tucked and her elbows on her knees supporting her chin. "Do you still visit her, Nonna?"

"No, no, I don't."

"Is she happy? What happened to her?"

I handed the necklace back to Rachel. "I don't know what became of her, and I don't know if she's happy. I certainly hope so, hummingbird. I hope so with all my heart."

My mind drifted back sixty-seven years.

CHAPTER 2

Charles Town 1764

On the day Hannah first saw Bintu, it was warmer than it had been, so she made sure to take her lighter hat, the one with the wide, flat brim. The days began chilly but would warm up as the day progressed, and the broader hat would shade her eyes from the sun when it bounced off the harbor water. As she walked down the aisle of her mother's shop, she tied it loosely under her chin in case an errant breeze tried to snatch it off her head when she was making her deliveries.

It was a beautiful spring day in Charles Town, a thriving seaport only equaled by Newport, Rhode Island. A sailors' and merchants' town, the main streets were wide enough for carriages, wagons, and horses making the transportation of goods from the busy ships in the harbor to the various shops and warehouses easier.

Cobble and brick streets were the foundation of the new buildings, their roofs reaching to the sky, joining the spires of the churches. The stucco-and-brick fronts of the homes imbued an air of elegance to the young city. Construction flourished as houses and buildings constantly sprouted. And this wasn't the first time Charles Town had built itself anew from the dust and ashes.

The citizens of Charles Town were careful to keep the streets free of debris as they'd learned their lesson from a conflagration years earlier. The city had nearly burned to the ground in a blaze started by a runaway hearth fire whose sparks rode the wind, jumping from house to house, decimating 300 abodes. The town had been rebuilt in brick or plaster; if the houses were built of wood, the owners needed to prove their chimney was made of stone, ensuring another runaway blaze would not escape from a hearth.

The biggest and most splendid house in this colony of South Carolina was Mistress Pinckney's, one of the very first built after the fire. It looked like a palace, and was for all intents and purposes. Overlooking Colleton Square on the north end of the bay, the Pinckneys' wide porch had a splendid view across the water to Sullivan's Island, a green hummock cast among the grey-green waters of Cooper River. Hannah liked to imagine herself on those balconies looking out to sea, waiting for her ships to arrive from Europe, the Caribbean, and even the Far East. Big ships full of interesting cargo from all over the world captained by brave men. The kind of ships that her papa often loaded with goods for the merchants' shops on Hassell Street, including her mother's shop.

Her mother's shop smelled like wood dust, vinegar, and coffee, the smell of Hannah's childhood. Really, it was her father's shop, but he was away so often that she thought of it only as her mother's. The shop's wares reflected her mother's talents as a seamstress, baker, and businesswoman. The cloth for sale was good quality but not overly expensive. Hannah's mother, Rebekah, had a talent of picking just the right type in just the right colors, a talent only exceeded by her ability to turn the fabrics into something stunning. Rebekah was also careful to carry only the best flour, spices, sugar, salt, and even yeast. When she was not selling them, she'd be close to her oven in the kitchen behind the house, baking one delicacy after another.

Hannah loved to make deliveries from her mother to the Pinckneys, and even though she'd never formally met the mistress of the house, the half-hour trip on foot was worth it. Mistress Pinckney had made many in Charles Town rich with her indigo, and she often traded at Rebekah's shop. Hannah had seen her there in her lovely deep-blue dresses and beautiful auburn hair piled on top of her head. Hannah could tell she was clever by the arch of her elegant eyebrows and the glint in her eye. Each time Hannah approached the grand house she had hoped to catch a glimpse of Mistress Pinckney on her balcony in her dressing gown.

And it was to the mistress' house that Hannah was headed that morning.

Normally, the Pinckneys would send one of their house slaves for the weekly order, but this week Mistress Pinckney had forgotten a crucial item, sugar, and so Rebekah sent Hannah to finish the delivery. Her mother knew Hannah loved getting out of the shop into the fresh air, and seeing the Pinckneys' grand house was thrilling for the young girl. Besides, it was a lovely morning.

Rebekah was packing the delivery basket as Hannah petted their old tom cat, King Sol, as he purred up at her from the counter. Suddenly, her mother paused in her packing and asked her what day it was. That struck Hannah as odd. Mama was so organized; why wouldn't she have remembered the date?

"Is it the third Thursday of the month?" Rebekah asked. "The twenty-third?"

Hannah did the mental calculations as she scratched the spot behind the cat's ears that he loved.

"Yes, Mama, it is." She itched King Sol harder and his purr intensified.

"Oh my." The woman studied the basket on the counter,

considering something. Then she looked up with a fierce expression. "You're not to go down to the wharves today, Hannah. You take the long way around to Mistress Pinckney's. Down King Street and across town. Like that."

"But, Mama," the girl protested, confused. She'd stopped petting the old cat who was now butting his head against her shoulder. "That will take twice the time! If I go by the wharves, then I'll—"

"I said to go the long way," her mother interrupted. "The ships are in, and there's too much going on."

"But—"

"I don't care how long the trip takes. Do not go down to those wharves. Promise me."

Hannah was speechless. Going all the way around would double her trip. While she deliberated, Mama reached out and grabbed her hand, hard enough to hurt a little, and hissed, "Promise!"

"All right, Mama," Hannah said, cringing. "I promise."

Rebekah's expression softened as she released the girl's hand. "It's not you, Hannah. It's just that there's a lot going on down there today, *gatinha,* and I don't want you getting mixed up in it."

Hannah's hands were tight on the handle of the basket. "What kind of things, Mama?" she asked warily.

"Not things for a thirteen-year-old girl to see, that's for certain. Cease asking questions, child, just do as I say." With that her mother stopped short, and turned her attention to the cat that had sprawled inelegantly across the wooden counter. King Sol really only fancied Hannah, and it made Rebekah furious. "And get that cat off of the counter. We serve food here!" Hannah obliged, scooping the orange cat onto the floor. He stalked off down the aisle after spearing Rebekah with a dark glance.

Hannah took this as a sign to leave, even though she was still awfully curious about what was happening at the wharves. Rebekah's expression was less exasperation and more wary fear, and that kept Hannah's questions bottled up.

When Hannah stepped out of the front door of Cardozo's Dry Goods, the bright morning sun hit her full in the face and she adjusted her hat brim. As she started down Hassell Street, the heavy basket pulled at her shoulder muscles so much that she realized that a longer route might be too much for her. She needed a shortcut. She thought she knew of one that would take her between the major thoroughfares of town, but still avoided the wharves as her mother had instructed. She thought about it for another moment and then, her jaw in a stubborn set her mother would have instantly recognized, she tightened her grip on the basket and set off.

Ten minutes later, she was on a narrow footpath between buildings that opened onto Broad Street. Her heart was racing. *I shouldn't be here.* For all her curiosity, she was not a girl to disobey such a strongly worded warning from her mother.

Hannah had taken the shortcut for its cool shadows as well as to save time and her aching shoulders. She'd thought it would put her farther along King Street. She'd been wrong, or gotten turned around somehow, because this alley had led her straight into the heart of the wharf district, opening up at Motte's Wharf.

The clatter of carriages and shouts of merchants drifted in from the docks as Hannah tentatively approached the mouth of the alley. She peeked out, mouse-like, and a breeze blew the smell of river silt and the sea into her face. The wharves bustled with people and the wooden docks were heaped with mountains of wares to be sold and traded. Usually this area was pretty quiet, with merchants, seamen, and the Crown's surveyors going about their daily routines. Today, the wharves bristled with masts from the ships jammed into the harbor, their crews crowding the docks.

Hannah was about to double-back down the alley, which would have added even more mileage to her trip, when she saw him. He was fast-walking across the cobblestones of the square. She only just glimpsed his white-tie wig with the black ribbon in the back as he walked toward the ships, his face hidden. Even though she had only seen his profile for a few heartbeats, she was certain it was her Uncle Aaron. She wanted to go after him, but it was against her mother's wishes, so she began to turn back, shoulders aching even more at the thought of her doubled footwork. Just as he was about to disappear into the swarm of men, he looked over his shoulder and Hannah got a good look at his expression.

His mouth was set in a line and brows creased, bringing them almost over his eyes. He looked worried and, for a moment, very uneasy. And even if Mama had expressly forbidden it and had made her promise, Hannah couldn't help herself. She had to follow Uncle Aaron. She had to see what agitated him.

Hannah stepped into the market square—a large open area studded with palmetto trees with horse-drawn carriages circling the perimeter—yelling "Uncle Aaron!" at his retreating back. Her shouts were to no avail, however, so she trotted to catch up.

She tried to keep him in view as he dodged between the throngs of people, but she stumbled over the curb, yanking her heavy delivery basket with her, and onto the grassy area bordering the promenade, which ran parallel to the sea. In the distance floated the hazy image of Sullivan's Island. After she had regained her balance and rested the basket at her feet for a beat, she looked for his tell-tale white wig with the black bow. She was suddenly struck by what was displayed in the middle of the disorderly crowd of men shouting and jostling for position. They all gave it a wide berth, like they were frightened of it, as if it were a wild caged beast. Hannah had never seen one before, but the large boxy shape in the middle of the group was instantly recognizable. And she finally understood why her mother had forbidden her to come here today. It all became clear to her in one hot rush.

It was the slave market, and the object of attention was an auction block to display slaves for sale above the crowd so that everyone could examine the wares. *That's why Mama forbade me from coming here, the slave market,* Hannah reasoned.

Although it was a common enough occurrence in Charles Town and was advertised freely, Mama didn't have a taste for slavery. She never had, which was putting it mildly. Her mother had shielded Hannah from the worst of it. The Cardozos didn't own enslaved people, which was unusual in Charles Town. Rebekah had taken every opportunity to steer her daughter away from the tawdry displays of abject cruelty that was the norm in Charles Town. The slave market also brought sailors, sellers, and other unsavory characters to shore and therefore was no place for a young girl.

Panic seeped into Hannah's bones as she desperately searched the crowd for Uncle Aaron, who would lead her away from this. He could get her out of here. Her mother would lash her with the sharp side of her tongue and worse if she found out Hannah had disobeyed her, but Hannah knew Uncle Aaron probably wouldn't tell. He could be trusted. That was one of the many reasons why he was her favorite uncle.

Hannah glimpsed him talking to a man just behind the auction block. The sight of them there together gave her pause, and she stopped next to a wagon wheel. There were a few wagons pulled up at the very edge of the crowd, most likely waiting to transport new acquisitions back to one of the many South Carolina plantations. The man Uncle Aaron was talking to was dressed in a tan suit with a wide brimmed hat, and holding a sheaf of papers. He looked like he was in charge. Hannah's breath hitched when she saw what was in his other hand—a long, cruel-looking switch.

Just then, another group was called up to the block, the previous souls having been sold, their destinies decided. There was an older man and woman clutching one another as they stepped onto the lowest of the block's three levels. Tears coursed down the old woman's face, following the deep lines etched there, but she was silent as she cried. A young woman with a baby on her hip hoisted herself onto the next tier. Finally, climbing up behind them and settling herself into a pose of regal indifference on the highest tier was a young girl about Hannah's age, skinny and tall. She was disheveled, her braids unraveling and her clothing, what little there was left, torn and stained, but she managed to remain aloof, standing as still as a statue on the auction block, and towering over the crowd. Her poise spoke of a refined upbringing and nerves of steel.

The sight of her knocked Uncle Aaron right out of Hannah's mind. There was something about that girl that looked so familiar, and yet new at the same time. Hannah felt instantly as if she'd known this girl all her life and simultaneously that she'd never seen anyone like her. In profile, the angle of the girl's nose and jaw mirrored one another, and her skin was glossy as polished stone.

As if she could feel Hannah's gaze, the girl turned to look at her. Her light blue eyes blazed out of the dark skin of her face. They were the color of the sea, the color of a summer sky. Hannah had never seen such an arresting color combination. She couldn't look away.

Wherever did she get those eyes? Hannah wondered.

The two girls stared at one another, the connection almost electric, until the man in charge stepped in between them.

"Lot thirty-six," he bellowed, using his long switch to point at the people on the auction block behind him.

The girl's eyes widened and she looked confused as the auctioneer spoke. Hannah doubted the girl could understand much of what he was saying, although it seemed as though she had some basic understanding. Periodically, she would squint at the man's face, and more specifically, his lips.

Hannah felt a sickening wave of relief when she realized that the girl probably couldn't understand that this man was extolling her virtues—what she could lift, how young she was, how many babies she might have as a "breeder," how stout her constitution—as if she were livestock.

According to the auctioneer, the blue-eyed girl was fresh off the

Final Passage from the West Indies and, before that, newly arrived from West Africa. He gestured to her arms and legs, and lastly, the auctioneer gestured to her face with his switch, narrowly missing her. She flinched.

"And those eyes, gentlemen," the auctioneer barked, "those eyes are the clearest blue I've seen in all my days of selling. One would never tire of such an extraordinary visage." The man reached up one beefy hand, his fingernails limned in black, and gripped the girl's chin hard enough that his fingertips indented her skin. She bucked her head, twisting it and trying to escape his grip, but he held firm. "A rare article here, those eyes. You won't see the like for sale again, I'll warrant that."

Murmurs of approval fluttered through the crowd.

"How much for this wench, then?" the overseer barked. "She is worth at least five hundred pounds. Do I hear five hundred?"

It was then that Hannah caught sight of Uncle Aaron across the heads of those between them. He was staring right at her, his face as dark as a rain cloud about to spend its fury. She turned, the delivery basket still gripped white-knuckled, and ran back the way she'd come.

CHAPTER 3
1831 Charleston, South Carolina

"**W**as Uncle Aaron mad at you, Nonna?" Rachel asked, prodding me to continue the story of the blue-eyed girl.

I was jolted back to the present by my granddaughter's question and by the fact that, out of everything she'd just been told, *this* was the question that occurred to the girl. I glanced at the face of the tall case clock standing against the wall behind the dining room.

"Come, hummingbird." I stood with some difficulty, feeling blood leave my head and surge into my legs. "We need to finish the challah in the kitchen house. It's time we braid and bake it. How many braids should we make, three or four? Three is for love, hope, and peace but the fourth is for loving arms. You choose."

"Let's do four." Rachel was right behind me as we walked to the back door and took down two shawls, wrapping them around our shoulders.

"Was he mad, Nonna? Your uncle? Was he very mad?"

We walked quickly across the small yard to the kitchen, which was in a different structure from the main house, just as it had been when I was a child. Nothing much had changed in all these years—except for me.

"No, Rachel, he wasn't. But we had to talk about it the next time we saw one another."

I began to take what I would need out of the cupboard. I'd made the dough earlier, and once the sun went down all work would cease. The sweet-smelling dough had finished rising in my mother's clay bowl in the chamber of the chimney, where it was warmest. Now it was time to braid it.

"When did you see him next?" Rachel took her accustomed spot next to me, stepping up onto her painted stool.

"It was at Friday services, a few days after." I pushed the large bowl, covered by cloth, toward her. "Wash your hands before you touch the dough, Rachel."

The girl turned to the basin, scrubbing at her hands and drying them on her apron. "At the synagogue? The one we go to with Mama?"

"Our synagogue wasn't built yet when I was a child. It was built in 1792. We used to meet at families' houses for services, Seder, and Shabbat."

"We have Shabbat dinners here," Rachel said.

"Yes, I know." From the sack I poured a circle of flour onto the board, spreading it with my fingertips. I plopped the shiny smooth dough on the board and began to work it with the heels of my hands, pushing it down and folding the ends in on itself.

"What did Uncle Aaron say to you the next time he saw you?" Rachel asked as she obediently kneaded the bread.

"He wasn't mad at *me*, but he was worried that *I* was mad at *him*."

My mind again returned to nearly seven decades earlier.

The Jewish families of Charles Town did not yet have a place to call their own. They didn't have a synagogue, they didn't even have a rabbi, but they had each other, and that was a start. They were luckier than many. Charles Town was a place where Jewish families could practice their faith. The charter itself even stated so in Article 19, and as a result, there was little prejudice toward Judaism. It was easy for Jews to find their niche in the community as long as they were willing to assimilate.

For Friday evening services and Shabbat morning, the small congregation would visit one another's houses on a revolving basis. On the Friday after Hannah saw her uncle at the slave auction, Shabbat evening services were held at the DaCostas' household.

The DaCostas were one of the most important families in the fledgling Jewish community. If anyone was close to being a rabbi, it was Isaac DaCosta. Well-educated and versed in the Scriptures, he had a natural command and respect from his friends and fellow businessmen. He was a serious man, but kind, and always welcomed new arrivals into his home.

The DaCostas were transplants to the colonies so their houses were not lavish; they displayed only a few select treasures that reminded them of their origins and their flight from Portugal and the Inquisition. The rest of the polished mahogany furnishings were well-chosen and beautifully made, imported from Europe—furnishings fit for merchants of means with an eye for value and style.

Late in the afternoon, Hannah and her family met the Lindos by the DaCostas' front gate. Each family greeted one another as they walked up the oyster-shell path to the house together, the men at the head, the women toting baskets or platters next, and the children last. Their feet crunched on the path's white shells.

There wasn't a Lindo child Hannah's age, but they had a girl about the same age as Hannah's younger brother, Levi. Levi and Mila weren't friends exactly; they were more like friendly enemies and their good-natured animosity kept gatherings lively. On the steps up to the DaCosta front door, they bumped into one another, literally, as Hannah, two steps ahead of them, tried to keep her pies steady.

The group squeezed through the narrow doorway and into the equally narrow front hallway of the DaCosta house. As on most other Friday evenings, the girls and women toted their baskets and platters out to the kitchen behind the house where Moira DaCosta and her daughters would be organizing the meal.

Hannah set the table, a task she volunteered for because she could eavesdrop on the men camped out across the hall in the parlor, tongues wagging about all sorts of Charles Town business.

As Hannah lay the cutlery and set out candles at intervals along the table, she listened to the men as they discussed the ebb and flow of fortune as it was delivered by ships from the West Indies and Europe on the tides of the Ashley and Cooper Rivers.

She was occupied with piling salt on a saucer (for dipping the challah bread) set in the middle of the table, only half-listening to the mellifluous burble of the men's talk as it floated across the hallway. One said the word "wharves," and Hannah's attention piqued. She could almost feel her ears swiveling to catch the rest of what he said.

"Yes, a lot of merchandise arrived at the wharves earlier this week," a familiarly gruff voice continued. "We'll be able to do well with the Windsor chairs, Madeira, and window glass. The ships arrived from Sullivan's Island with forty lots." Hannah pictured Master DaCosta with his kindly brown eyes peering out of his round face. "Aaron Lopez was our man at the wharves."

"I thought Lopez predominantly dealt in whale oil," another said. "He was there for the slaves?"

Hannah froze with one hand hovering halfway to the table. Slavery was nothing new to her, but after her turn at the auction, she felt sick about what that girl's fate might've been. She was troubled about her uncle's presence, too. Why was he there? Was her uncle dealing in slaves? She knew it was none of her business, but it still bothered her to think about it, and she wasn't sure why.

"His primary business is in spermaceti candles. He and his

brother Moses built a very successful candle factory. Unfortunately, the slave business wasn't as kind to him."

"I heard he almost lost his hat," someone said, and the other men laughed.

After this, the conversation took a turn for the boring, and Hannah's mind wandered back to the young slave girl she'd seen on the auction block. She was setting out the pewter trenchers they used as plates with the face of the blue-eyed, dark-skinned girl in her mind. She'd thought about her a dozen times since she'd first seen her, and the men's conversation had brought her to the forefront of Hannah's thoughts again.

Hannah's mother called to her from the doorway and soon she was absorbed back into the preparations for the Shabbat dinner with no time to think of Uncle Aaron or the girl on the block.

After services it was time for the lighting of the candles. The three families gathered around as Moira lit the candles, waving her arms over the new flames as if she were gathering the light to her face, and covering her eyes for a moment of reflective prayer. When she finished, she smiled widely, gesturing up and down the table for all to sit.

Hannah was seated in the middle section of the long wooden table, in between the adults and the children. She could tune into the adults when she could hear over the uproarious laughter from the kids' section. It seemed her little brother, Levi, was quite humorous.

After the adults had blessed the wine and then the challah, the bread was uncovered, broken into chunks, dipped into salt, and passed down the long length of the table on its wooden trencher. It was during this ritual that the sound of the front door opening made everyone look expectantly toward the hallway.

A man's voice called out, "Tobias? Isaac?"

Hannah's heart filled with dread. Usually when she heard Uncle Aaron's voice she would be up and out of her chair in an instant, running to be the first to hug him. Not tonight, though. Tonight she felt wary, as if he were a stranger to her.

Isaac greeted Aaron from his seat, asking him to come in and join them. The front door scraped again over the wooden floorboards. When he entered the dining room, Aaron glanced pointedly at Hannah, his long olive face concerned, but he didn't say anything to her. Instead, he walked around the table to his host, Isaac, and shook his hand.

"Shabbat Shalom, Aaron," old Isaac said as he pumped the younger man's hand up and down. "Please, take a seat. We've saved some challah and wine for you."

Aaron sat, much to the chagrin of the four children clustered around him, and glanced once more at Hannah before accepting a piece of challah from Moira and a sip of wine from the shared cup.

Conversation flowed again, centering on a school Hannah had never heard them talk about—a school for Negro children, a school for slaves run by a slave, a man named Harry.

"Slaves are forbidden to learn to read or write, yet the most prominent members of St. Philips invest in a school that does just that," Matthew said. "They built that building that Harry teaches in and bought him to work in it, years ago. If there's something in it for them, the parish tends to overlook the laws, even if it was they who made them."

"Don't they worry that educating their slaves might lead to an uprising, like the Stono Rebellion?" Isaac asked. "That was just down the road. White slave owners were killed and, in retaliation, those who rebelled were executed and their heads put on fence posts leading into Charles Town. So many lost their lives. Many blame the slaves learning their letters."

"That's the common idea. If you teach your slaves to read and write, you're asking for trouble."

Aaron shrugged. "Some believe the benefits outweigh the costs. It makes business sense to educate the slaves. We have a real need for skilled craftsmen here in Charles Town, and educated slaves can fill that gap."

"The idea was proposed by The Society for the Propagation of the Gospel in Foreign Parts," Isaac intoned. "They sent early missionaries from The Church of England to the colonies. They thought educated slaves made better workers. That's all changing now as some newcomers are not so inclined."

"And if those workers are still slaves, no one has to pay them," Tobias added, eliciting nods from the men around him. "No matter *how* skilled they are."

Hannah caught sight of her mother's face and the look of disgust that quickly changed into a studied interest of her plate.

"The slaves can be taught to read but *not* to write," Isaac clarified, "to stop the spread of ideas. The Negro Act of 1740 is very clear. If slaves are caught writing or teaching others to write, they're punished. Severely."

Hannah's appetite vanished. For the first time in her mostly comfortable life, she considered the fact that, if she were enslaved, she could be punished, maybe even killed, for the simple act of writing, a skill she'd been taught as soon as she was capable. It made her feel nauseated. It was a foreign, heavy idea, and it rankled, like a piece of corn stuck between her molars.

After dinner, Uncle Aaron found her as she was emptying slops for the chickens and the wily nanny goat the DaCostas kept in a pen out back. She'd flung the dry bits of food to the hens and was pouring the rest of the bucket into the trough when she heard a step behind her.

"Hannah."

It took her a moment to answer him with cool deference. "Good evening, Uncle Aaron. What can I do for you?"

Even in the gloaming, the older man's face was pinched. Hannah's tone was frigid. "I know you saw me at the wharves yesterday. I want to talk to you about it. To explain."

"No need to explain anything, Uncle. I understand."

"You do?" He sounded surprised. The two fell silent and the goat's snuffling and the women's muted laughter and conversation from inside the DaCostas' dining room filled the space between them. "What exactly do you understand?"

"I understand that it's business, if it's whale oil, or indigo, or slaves. And it's not my place to question the affairs of men's business."

Aaron nodded as a soft spring breeze swept through the small yard, rustling the magnolia trees and unleashing their dusty violet scent. "That sounds like your father speaking."

Hannah did not reply. She didn't understand exactly why she felt angry and upset, but she did. Her stomach was queasy with it.

"That's good then, isn't it?" Hannah murmured, keeping her eyes pinned to her feet, not wanting to meet her uncle's gaze. "I'm supposed to obey my father and learn from him, aren't I?"

"But that's not the Hannah I know." He tried to reach out to touch her shoulder, but she shrugged him off. "Are you angry?"

"It . . . it just seems so unfair. To them. The slaves." Hannah spoke quietly, not accusingly, just curious, even though her stomach was twisting with emotion.

"I see," Uncle Aaron said. "Hannah, your mother has never agreed with the practice of slavery. In fact, she despises it. Your family, as I'm sure you've noticed, has never had slaves. That in itself isn't that unusual among our people, but your mother in particular is averse. She calls it inhuman. And so, she has protected you from some of the common practices. It would be impossible for you to live here in Charles Town and not be familiar with it, but you are more removed than most children your age."

"Uncle Aaron," Hannah sniffed, pride stung. "I am not a child anymore. These are not the affairs of children."

That gave him pause for a moment, and he stroked his chin. "That is true; I can see that now. But let me assure you that what you saw at the wharves is a monthly, even weekly, event in Charles Town."

"The auction?"

"Yes, they bring in lots—slaves—from Sullivan's Island when the ships are in and there is a surplus. Auctions take place like clockwork."

"And you're a part of it. That's why I saw you there."

Aaron nodded. "I am a merchant. However, slavery is not my primary business. My company makes candles from spermaceti. We tried our hand at the slave trade, but the winds of fortune did not blow our way."

After a few moments, Hannah asked, "Even though you're a part of it, doesn't mean I have to agree with it?"

Aaron's eyes glinted like light flashing on silver. "I've always told your mother that shielding you wouldn't help you in the long run. Not even a little." He leaned down to look her directly in the eyes. "Listen to me, Hannah. I will not tell you what to believe. But I will tell you to hold your tongue. Speaking like that to adults, asking those kinds of questions, it will only bring trouble on your head."

Hannah's arms erupted with goosebumps.

"You have your mother's fire, but I'm afraid such fire will only burn you." Her uncle turned and walked back to the kitchen.

On their trip home from the DaCostas, Hannah was silent and thoughtful. Her mother tried and failed to engage her in light conversation, so she wrapped her arm around the girl's slim waist, and they walked in silence to the building that housed their store and living quarters above.

That night, Rebekah came into Hannah's room as Hannah was trying to get a comb through her impossible curls. She took the comb from her daughter's hands and began to gently tug it through the stubborn knots.

"I saw you speaking with your uncle, *gatinha*. Did he say anything to upset you?"

Hannah's eyes stung, both from the memory of her conversation with Uncle Aaron and the pain of the comb in her curls. She shook her head and concentrated on the flame flickering in the oil lamp on her bedside table.

"All right. You don't have to tell me if you don't want to," her mother said. "But know that I am always here if you need me."

CHAPTER 4

Monday morning dawned sunny with a light breeze, and no chance of rain. The spring weather normally lifted Hannah's spirits, but she was still thinking about her conversation with her uncle and was feeling conflicted from all the revelations of the days before. When Hannah had completed her toilet, she went down the rickety wooden stairs into the store to find that Levi had already left and her mother was behind the counter, finishing preparations for another delivery basket. Hannah was surprised.

"Another delivery, Mama?" Hannah took the cloth-wrapped cornbread from her mother, holding it up to her face and inhaling the steam. "What about my studies?"

"I've postponed them. I have a different kind of instructive lesson planned for you today."

Hannah's eyebrows raised, breakfast forgotten.

"You're to deliver this basket to this address." She handed Hannah a scrap of paper.

"Where is this?" Hannah scrunched up her nose as she read the address. "I don't think I've delivered there before, Mama."

"You haven't. Usually, I do the delivery. It is in the glebe lands near the two big Christian Churches."

Rebekah never made the deliveries, or so Hannah had believed. "*You* do the deliveries? *You?*"

Her mother stayed silent. Hannah looked down at the small crock of preserve she had taken from the basket. The things in there were all luxury items, a chunk of sweet-smelling soap, a few candles, honey, and a set of sewing needles and thread. There was even a small ginger cake. These weren't items Hannah typically found in her delivery baskets. Usually, it was basic staples—bags of flour and sugar, tins of molasses. This delivery was more like gifts than goods.

"Now you know where you are going, correct? Coming Street," her mother clarified. "Go east through town, turn left by the church, and then again at the Bryans' house. It's at the end of that street. A small yellow house with windows on one side and a kitchen in the back." Hannah's mother flapped her apron at her daughter, shooing her toward the door. "Deliver that, and be back for lunch."

And so once again Hannah found herself headed out with yet another basket, this one destined for a mystery address. And she wasn't alone; this time King Sol accompanied her, trotting beside her like an imperial guard.

After a series of twists and turns with King Sol at her heels, Hannah finally stood on Coming Street in front of a small yellow house. She checked the scrap of paper one more time, making sure that the number her mother had written matched the number on the gate. It did.

The houses here were modest except for the churches of St. Philips and St. Michaels, both impressive and imposing. They looked like two sentinel giants keeping watch over the smaller homes clustered around their steps. Hannah straightened her bonnet and secured the flowered cloth over the contents of the basket. She looked down at King Sol, sitting majestically at her feet. He was a magnificent specimen of a tom cat with long ragged orange hair and a permanently disdainful expression in his orange eyes.

"You stay here, Sol, keep watch." Then she marched up the front path and knocked on the door, white paint flaking off with each strike of her knuckles.

In a moment, the door was opened by a dark-skinned boy about Levi's age in coarse blue clothing that hung too loosely on his gaunt frame; it looked more like sacking than clothing. He grinned widely and made room for Hannah to enter without asking who she was.

"Teacher!" he hollered. "Delivery!" The boy shut the door behind Hannah and returned to a table that took up most of the space in the rectangular room.

Hannah realized that she was in a schoolhouse, much like the one that Levi attended on the days the siblings weren't needed at the store. It was a long, narrow room with a row of windows set low along one wall to let in light. Louvers were set on the opposite side to let in air. A door at the back opened onto a yard where Hannah could glimpse an outdoor kitchen. Air and sunlight flowed through the open back door, with dust motes floating lazily through the slats of light.

Stone slate boards were piled up against the wall to Hannah's right. In lieu of desks there was one large, battered worktable. *Like an old man-o-war*, Hannah thought. The table stood in the middle of the room with two benches pulled up to either side of it. Children of all ages, mostly boys, all of them Black, were seated at the table. Hannah suddenly understood that they were slaves. She could tell from the type of clothing that they wore. They wore "Negro cloth"— coarse, uncomfortable material that was the only thing slaves were allowed to dress themselves in. The children stayed bent over their studies. And one little boy gave Hannah a shy smile then went back to his laborious reading.

From the back doorway, a man appeared with a dishcloth, wiping his hands as he strode across to where Hannah stood with her basket. He was tall and willowy and well-dressed in a homespun mustard waistcoat and soft cotton breeches. He did not wear Negro cloth. He was light skinned, with a reddish tinge to his hair. His face was long and his eyes, when they settled on her, were wary. *There's something about his eyes,* Hannah thought. Something that reminded her of stained-glass windows.

When he reached her, he didn't immediately say anything but stood studying her. She shifted from one foot to the other. *Is he waiting for me to say something?*

"You're not Mistress Cardozo," the man said finally.

"No, I'm not. I'm her daughter." Hannah's arms ached from the basket, but the man hadn't invited her to put it down.

"Yes, you are, aren't you? I could tell. Here, follow me. You can put the basket out in the kitchen house." The man turned to lead her across to the door he'd come through.

"Oh!" he spun toward her, and with a huge grin that transformed his former wariness into something much more welcoming, he said, "I'm Harry."

Hannah grinned back. "I am Hannah."

"Nice to meet you, Miss Hannah. And this," he said, opening his arms, "this is my school."

Hannah's guess had been right. This was the school they'd been talking about during Shabbat, the school that educated slaves and the children of slaves. The Negro Act of 1740 dictated that no slaves were to be educated in the colony of South Carolina and, if there were a school, the person in charge could be whipped and fined. So how could this school be open? How did Harry teach these children? How did her mother know so much about Harry and what he did here? If her mother knew so much, why did Hannah herself know so little?

Hannah's curiosity was getting the better of her as she stole glances around the schoolroom. It was impeccably clean. There was a stack of simple Bibles on the table, their covers worn with use. Next to them was a stack of primers like the one Levi used when he was learning the alphabet. The paper covers were tattered, and the pages stained from many hands.

As she followed Harry across the schoolroom's uneven floorboards, she thought, *Mother regularly delivers here. Will wonders never cease?*

Harry led Hannah through a narrow doorway and down two broad stone steps into the backyard and the kitchen. It was so hot for so many months in Charles Town that most residents had kitchens in their backyards to avoid unnecessarily heating up the insides of their homes. Sometimes kitchens were separate buildings with tables and chairs and workspaces, and in others, like this one, there was just a hearth with basic tools and an old worktable and a rickety roof to keep out the worst of the rain.

The stone steps led to the dirt yard where sturdy wooden posts had been set in the earth about five feet apart and rising seven feet, with a cypress shingled roof covering the area in between to make a covering. Three of the structure's sides were constructed of rough yellow pine planks, reaching high enough to block wind and rain but open enough to still give the kitchen ventilation.

Bright sunlight made Hannah squint. Harry was moving a pile of sweet potatoes from the table to a bin underneath it to make room for Hannah's basket. His eyes were slate grey, shot through with brown. Another figure—a girl—had her back to them as she scrubbed a pot in the basin next to the pump. The girl's dark hair was pinned back behind her head in whorls and braids, and she was wearing the same shapeless clothing as the others. In the bright light, Hannah could see that the girl's dress was ornamented in some way, as if someone had embroidered patterns onto the loosely woven cloth.

Hannah placed her basket on the spot Harry indicated, and the girl at the basin turned. That's when Hannah got her second shock of the morning. The girl's blue eyes lit up in the sun when she glanced with uncertainty at Hannah, making them cerulean in her dark face.

It was the blue-eyed girl from the auction block. The girl took the preserves and honey from Hannah with a shy smile, and Hannah smiled back.

"Hannah, this is Bintu," Harry said. "Bintu, this is Hannah."

"Pleased to meet you," Hannah said.

Bintu put her hand over her heart and bowed. "Pleased," she said haltingly.

"Delighted," Hannah said.

Up close, Hannah could see that Bintu had embroidered, bunched, and tied parts of her sack-like dress so that it gathered a bit at her waist and the sleeves nipped in. It made the garment look less like a burlap sack and more like a dress, one that, if not exactly fashionable, was a sight better than what the others were made to wear.

Bintu and Hannah finished unpacking together, and Bintu folded the cloth that had covered the wares in the basket, handing it back to Hannah, who tucked it away. After a moment of awkward silence, Hannah turned to Harry to lead her back out toward the street. Her mother would be expecting her for lunch.

As Harry led, Hannah followed him with her empty basket in hand and Bintu just behind them. As soon as they were inside, Bintu bobbed a curtsey and hurried to sit with the boys at the table. As Hannah tied her bonnet at the doorway, Harry began speaking to her.

"Chastity is Bintu's new name, I suppose. Her slave name." He wrinkled his nose for a moment, and then his face smoothed out again. "She doesn't know her new name yet. In fact, she doesn't know much English at all, except for what she learned on the ships. She just got here from West Africa. She is *Senegambian*. They say they make the most obedient slaves," Harry said in a voice edged in steel.

"I know. I've seen her before," Hannah blurted.

"You saw her?" Harry replied. "Where?"

"At the slave market the other day, and Bintu—I mean Chastity— was there, on the block." Suddenly something occurred to Hannah, and she looked at Harry, blood rushing to her cheeks. "Please don't tell my mother that I was there! I wasn't supposed to be there, and she doesn't know."

"No, no, of course not. I won't say anything to Mistress Cardozo, Miss Hannah." Harry studied her with an interest. "But hopefully we get to see you again? Tell me, do you like teaching? Working with children?"

"I surely do, Mister Harry!" Hannah said, relieved that he didn't seem inclined to tattle on her. "Well, unless my student is my brother Levi. He's impossible."

"I wonder. Do you think your mother might let you come help out here in the next few weeks? A couple of hours each morning?"

"To help teach?"

"To teach Bintu," Harry clarified. "Bintu needs to learn English quickly if she's going to survive."

Bintu was studying one of the primers with a much younger child. The size difference between Bintu, who was long and tall like Hannah, and the young boy at her side was almost comical. *I wonder if she knows we're talking about her.*

"I would teach the girl myself," Harry continued, "but I have the young ones, and classes for their parents in the evenings. Bintu is so smart; she's picking up every lesson I put in front of her. Someday I hope she'll teach the little ones with me, but first someone has to teach her."

"I don't know." Hannah was flattered, but she'd need permission. "I'd have to ask my mother, of course."

"Yes, of course." Harry led her to the door. "Give me an answer as soon as you can."

Hannah fairly skipped all the way home, King Sol trotting a few steps behind, so excited was she at the prospect of helping teach at Harry's School.

CHAPTER 5

That afternoon, Rebekah closed the store for lunch and she and Hannah retired to the back garden for their meal. The kitchen house was a nice respite from the bustle and heat of the store and the constant questions from customers. Hannah loved the kitchen because it always smelled of nutmeg and baked bread, and it was a shady escape from the hot Carolina sun.

The front of the building was open, and the back wall had louvers for air circulation. The wide, rough-hewn boards of the floor and walls were shiny with wear and the combination of spills and polishing over the years. The large hearth was at one end with the bread oven built into the chimney. A sturdy table provided a workspace as well as a place for lunch or tea, and three equally sturdy chairs made up the rest of the furniture.

Stepping into the basic structure that made up their kitchen house, Hannah joined her mother, who was tending the fire and heating up soup in a big iron pot that hung on a crane over the flames. Rebekah reached back to grab the cornbread wrapped in cloth off the kitchen table.

"Let me do it, Mama," Hannah said, gently but firmly pushing down on her mother's shoulders until the older woman sank into a chair. Rebekah made one futile sound and then sighed and stretched her feet toward the small fire, worn leather shoes peeking out from beneath her long skirt.

"Ah, that feels nice. Thank you, Hannah." Rebekah closed her eyes and the tension drained from her face, smoothing out the lines around her mouth and softening her eyes. Hannah put the wrapped cornbread into the warming chamber in the chimney. "Tell me, what did you think of my friend Harry and his school?"

Hannah considered how to respond. Rebekah wouldn't jump at the idea of her teaching at Harry's school. She needed Hannah's help in the store most days, and it wasn't seemly for a young girl to be gallivanting all over town, even if it was for a good cause and most of the roaming was done in broad daylight.

Hannah, however, was thrilled with the idea of teaching Bintu. It was an opportunity to spread her wings outside the tight confines of their house and the store, the two places that occupied most of her existence. Hannah knew her mother only wanted what was best for her, but she also was beginning to realize that what her mother thought best wasn't always what Hannah had in mind.

"I thought a lot of Harry," Hannah said, gathering her skirts and squatting to watch the cornbread so it wouldn't burn. "And the students, they're all slaves?"

"Yes, they are."

Hannah poked the bread with her peel. Not ready yet. "The students are taught to read but not to write. Is that true?"

Rebekah opened one eye to look with amusement at her daughter. "Yes, my little bat with the big ears, that's what those in charge have dictated."

Hannah stood and took a slender spoon down from the wall. Lifting the cover off an iron pot with the hem of her skirt, she stirred the bubbling bean stew, aromatic steam wafting around her face.

"Don't forget the bottom, Hannah. Scrape it well. And yes, the students are taught to read but not to write. They learn to read using the Scriptures, but only the New Testament. The Old Testament, what we use, is forbidden."

"Why?"

"Because the Old Testament has stories such as Moses leading the slaves out of bondage and the parting of the Red Sea, but the New Testament is about resurrection and a rewarding afterlife for the obedient. It helps justify—" Rebekah stopped short.

Hannah scraped the bottom of the pot to loosen the stuck beans. "And how did Harry get to the school?"

"Harry and Abraham were two young slaves bought by the church years ago; they were fourteen when they were bought to teach in the school. Or that's the story anyway. "

"It seems so strange."

"Strange?"

"Just that—" Hannah tapered off, searching for words. "Just that I was taught to write as well as read, and yet those students, those children, won't get the chance to write. Because of some law."

"Yes, well, men make and abide by strange laws sometimes."

Hannah reached for the stoneware bowls in the open cupboard as well as a trencher to hold the cornbread.

"The cornbread, Hannah, don't let it burn," Rebekah said, still with her eyes closed. "I can smell it."

Hannah plunked bowls on the kitchen table and leapt to the hearth, grabbing up cornbread in a hand wrapped in a skirt just as the surface of each had turned a deep brown. Hannah tossed them on the table, where they steamed. She then sat, handing a spoon across the table to her mother. This was the moment to make her case.

"Harry asked me to do something for him, Mama, and I'd like to, with your permission."

Rebekah's spoon stopped halfway to her mouth. She put it back in her bowl, untasted. "Oh?"

"There's a girl at his school about my age, a slave. Her name's Bintu. She's just arrived from . . . wherever she came from," Hannah said awkwardly. "Harry wants me to teach her English."

Rebekah cocked her head. It was hard to read her reaction. "Does he now?"

"We took to one another," Hannah said, trying to keep the excitement from seeping into her voice. "Right away. She's to become a teacher too, at Harry's School, but first she needs to learn English. Harry asked me to be her tutor."

"He asked you?" Rebekah said, her soup cooling in front of her. "How long does he want you there? You have chores here too. I need you in the store."

Hannah inwardly groaned. *So far this is not going well.* "He said he wanted her to learn English as soon as possible. He thought a few hours a day for the next few weeks."

Rebekah considered the idea but shook her head. "I'm sorry, *gatinha*, it's too dangerous. Harry is lucky it has gone as smoothly as it has, but with all the recent unrest over the new taxes and the most recent appointment to governor, as well as the late arrival of Reverend and Mistress Harte, his school is a magnet for trouble. It's too dangerous. And I need you at the store."

"But Mama," Hannah's eyes stung with disappointment. "Please! I'm good at teaching. Look at Levi! He's smart—when he listens. And it's not dangerous. It's just children and Harry there. It would be in the middle of the day, in broad daylight. I would wake up early to help with the store, and then stay later in the evening. Please?"

Rebekah mulled this, but after a few moments studying the soup, she shook her head. "No, Hannah. I can't have you in danger. There will be other opportunities."

"Mama, please! It's not so much to ask, it's only—"

Rebekah smacked her hand on the table, making the remaining bread jump on the trencher. "No more! I've told you my decision. That's it, there's nothing more to talk about."

Hannah jammed her lips together, anger and disappointment dampening her hunger. The two didn't say much for the rest of their lunch, each sitting uneasily stirring their uneaten soups. Hannah continued her tasks for the rest of the day with a weighted heart. It felt like the inside of her mother's store was all of the world she was ever going to see. She looked around at the tightly packed shelves and sighed. Then she continued measuring out flour from the larger hogshead barrels into smaller, more manageable sacks.

When Uncle Aaron came the following night for dinner, as he did frequently when he was in town on business, the house was "pleasantly active," the description Rebekah used. To Hannah, it was downright chaotic.

The Levinsons' two youngest were being cared for by Rebekah that afternoon, four-year-old twin boys, so when Rebekah said, "pleasantly active," she did so with a wild look in her eyes, tousled hair, and a smear of flour across her cheek.

When Uncle Aaron entered the back garden by the gate, the last rays of daylight were leaving their street adrift in purple twilight, the woodsmoke from the cooking fires mingling with the scent of silt and salt water.

Hannah was helping with dinner at the outside table and Rebekah was chasing down Joseph and Leon. He walked down the stone path to the kitchen house and the cluster of hearth, table, and chairs, and sat. Hannah plunked the stew pot on the table and got ready to ladle it into bowls, a dark brown apron covering her dress to protect it from splatter and anything the Levinson boys might throw at her.

"Hello, niece," Uncle Aaron said, leaning over and taking a long whiff of the stew. "Mmmmm. Chicken?"

"Hello, Uncle Aaron," Hannah said with genuine affection. Any awkward feelings between them had disappeared. "Duck tonight. Master Levinson brought over a brace when he dropped off the twins this morning." Hannah stuck the peel, a long wooden tool she used to move things around in the hot hearth, under the loaf of brown bread sitting next to an earthenware pot of beans, pulling it out and depositing it deftly on the table behind her.

"Is that so?" he said, eyeing the food. "And my sister? Where is she this evening?"

Hannah began hacking at the bread with a long, serrated knife. "She's chasing the goblins somewhere."

When she looked at her uncle, he had a confused expression. "Goblins?" he asked. "Your mother is chasing fantastical creatures around the house?"

She laughed. "I mean Leon and Joseph, the Levinson twins. Mother is looking after them until tomorrow. She calls them the goblins because they're so . . . um, active."

"Mischievous, maybe," Aaron snorted, grabbing a handful of pecans from the basket in the middle of the table and the alligator nutcracker, a wedding present for Rebekah. He cracked the tough nuts in the ornate metal jaws, tossing the shells out beyond the kitchen steps to the ground. "Anything interesting this week?"

Hannah glanced at her uncle. *Perhaps,* she thought, *Uncle Aaron could be my ally?* "Mother sent me on a delivery the other day."

"Mmm . . . hmmm. Doesn't she do that nearly every day?"

"Yes, but this one was special. She sent me to Coming Street." Hannah watched over her shoulder for any flicker of recognition registered on his face.

"Coming Street, eh?" He looked up at her sharply, and his hands stopped fiddling with the nutcracker. "That school?"

She nodded.

"Well, well," Aaron leaned back in his chair, brushing nut shells from the front of his shirt, showing a mix of amusement and apprehension. "Who would've thought she'd send you there?"

Hannah pulled the pot beans halfway out and gave them a quick stir, pushing the earthenware pot back in to continue heating.

"And?" he asked. "What did you think of Harry and his students?"

"They're slaves, is that right? That's what Mama said. And I could tell because of their clothes."

"Yes, you would notice that, wouldn't you?"

"Well, Mama let me know what to look for. She said . . . " Hannah glanced around for her mother but saw they were still alone. "She said she was trying to make me less naive."

Aaron nodded as he separated the nuts from the shells. "And Harry?"

"I like Harry very much!" Hannah's voice escalated as she sensed an opening. "He asked for my help. He wants me to come to teach, a few days a week," she said in a rush, "to teach one of them, a girl about my age."

"Is that so? And what do you think?"

"I would love to." Hannah's face fell. "But Mama won't let me. She says it's too dangerous."

"Everywhere is dangerous in the colonies right now," Aaron muttered, more to himself than to her.

"It's her, the blue-eyed slave, the one that was on the auction block the day I saw you."

Aaron blinked at her. "Is it?"

"That's who Harry wants me to teach. Her name is Bintu—well, Chastity now. She got renamed when she was bought, you know. Harry said that's how it works."

"Yes, I do know. I know how it works."

Sensing that this was her moment, Hannah put her peel down and rushed around the table to him, grabbing his sleeve. "Oh please, Uncle Aaron, talk to her! I would love to get out of the store and this house. I'm so cooped up, and Bintu seemed nice, as did Harry. It would be fun to be around children instead of on my own so much. Even if they are slaves." Her voice faltered on the last word.

"I imagine you will be very good as a teacher, Hannah,"

"Thank you, Uncle Aaron," Hannah said. "They have a right to learn and it would be a way for me to contribute. Like . . . like," she struggled for a minute, trying to remember, her mouth working. "*Tzedek*! Isn't that what we learned from the Torah? 'Justice, justice you shall pursue.' Isn't that the line?"

"*Tzedek*, is it?" Aaron's face changed. "Lord knows Harry and his school deserve more righteous deeds." Aaron rubbed his clean-shaven chin and studied his niece. "Maybe we should do more than just deliver surprise baskets of dry goods. Maybe it's time we did something lasting. Be assured, I will speak to her about it. It might be an opportunity for both you and for us, as a community, to contribute something to people who have only seen unkindness on these shores."

CHAPTER 6

A ll throughout dinner, Hannah waited for Uncle Aaron to bring up the subject of Harry's school. She dutifully fielded requests from the twins, passing them bits of bread and refilling their trenchers or drinking cups when they needed it, all along watching Uncle Aaron out of the corner of her eye and willing him to make his move.

When she and Levi were clearing, Uncle Aaron gave her a little nod as she took his trencher, and turned his chair to fully face his sister. Rebekah had a rag on Leon's face, cleaning smeared food.

"Rebekah," Aaron began. Hannah felt a trill of anxiety run up her spine. Her grip on the trencher tightened.

"Oh, come on, Leon, be still, child!" Rebekah said, dipping one corner of her apron into a cup of water and scrubbing at the wriggling boy's face.

"Rebekah." Aaron reached out to still her hand.

She stopped, eyes wide.

"Hannah told me you had her deliver to Harry's school yesterday."

Hannah froze near the basin with her back to them, too scared and hopeful to watch the exchange.

"Yes," her mother said as Leon squirmed out of her grasp and took off, bare feet slapping down the flagstones and out of the garden gate, closely followed by his brother, also at top speed and volume. "Levi, follow the goblins . . . I mean Joseph and Leon. Please!"

After Levi had loped out of the garden after them, Rebekah turned her attention back to Aaron, who was waiting. "Why did you send her to the school, Rebekah?"

Surprised, Rebekah's eyes flicked to Hannah, understanding in a moment that something had gone on between Hannah and Aaron. "Well," she drew out the word, smoothing her apron before she answered. "To introduce her to some other people in our community. Different people. I thought if she met Harry, she might start to understand aspects of Charles Town that I haven't taught her about yet."

"Like slavery."

Hannah chanced a look at her mother's face. It was tight and uncomfortable. "Yes, like slavery," Rebekah agreed. When she met Hannah's gaze, her eyes flashed with anger. Rebekah did not like being cornered. "I haven't talked to her much about the subject. Frankly, I've avoided it. I thought if she met other children, and Harry, who is smart and kind, it would be a good way to start the conversation."

Aaron nodded. Rebekah gestured for Hannah to come sit beside her. The girl obliged, drying her dripping hands on her apron and sliding onto the small bench next to her.

"She told me Harry offered her a position to teach there."

Rebekah's eyes blazed fire for one moment, but then she reached out for her daughter's hand. "Yes, that's right."

"But you've denied her request," Aaron said gently. He was the diplomat of the family.

"You know why, Aaron." Hannah saw a vein pulse in her mother's temple. "It's too dangerous. The whole town is a powder keg, waiting for a spark. I can't have my girl in the middle of that."

"We're already in the middle of it," Aaron countered. "Hannah teaching there might help to show Harry and his students that there are people in our community, the Jewish community here in Charles Town, who value education for everyone—slaves as well as free people."

Rebekah snorted, more defensive than derisive. "And how could Hannah teaching at Harry's school show them that?"

"She could listen to what Harry says, about what's going on. It could be very important. Also, the girl herself has reasons to go there, beyond that she wants to get out of the house." Aaron nodded at Hannah.

Hannah turned to her mother. Rebekah looked weary, but not angry and stubborn as she had before.

"Mama," Hannah said, trying to match Uncle Aaron's gentle tone. "I thought it could be like practicing *Tzedek*—an act of justice. Isn't that what you taught me? If I was there, teaching, it would mean more to them than simply a basket of goods. Teaching Bintu—I mean Chastity—would be like giving them another teacher."

Rebekah took a deep breath, and exhaled slowly. "*Gatinha*, it's dangerous for a young girl out on her own in an unfamiliar place. Who knows what could happen?"

"But I wouldn't be on my own! You know Harry. You like him, you said so yourself." Hannah tried to keep her voice even, like her uncle's. She looked at him now and he gave her an encouraging nod. "They're not strangers. I already saw Bintu at the wharves when—" Hannah's eyes bulged, and she sucked in her breath. She had been so intent on presenting a solid argument that she'd forgotten to keep her excursion to the wharves a secret.

"What? Wharves?" Rebekah's eyes were on fire as she did the mental calculations. "When were you at the wharves? Was it the other day, when I forbade you to go?" Her mother's voice grew sharp, outrage just below the surface. Hannah stayed quiet, twisting her apron in her lap. "Do you mean to tell me that you went down to the wharves when I'd forbidden you, Hannah? Answer me!"

"Rebe—" Aaron started, but Rebekah raised her hand, silencing him.

Hannah was heartsick. She'd ruined her chances. There was no way her mother would let her teach at Harry's now. "Yes, Mama. I'm sorry. I got lost and I found myself there." Hannah chanced a look up at her mother's face. The fire was roaring in her mother's eyes now. Hannah flinched. "I'm sorry," she whispered.

"You could've been hurt, Hannah," Rebekah said so quietly she was almost imperceptible. Deadly quiet.

Aaron jumped in. "But I was there, and I made sure she was all right. You can't hide it from her any longer. She's no longer a child, and she'll come to understand her world one way or another. How do you want her to find out? By observing slave auctions, or with Harry at his school, with other children?"

That arrow found its mark. Rebekah sat with her head lowered, not responding, and then stood and moved away from the table. Aaron and Hannah looked at one another, not sure how to take this. Aaron offered his niece a small shrug.

Nobody spoke for minutes. They could hear Levi and the goblins in the small lane behind the house, and the rustle of the fruit trees in the garden, their lovely aroma mixing with the hint of a spring shower to come. When Rebekah turned back to them, her eyes were no longer angry; they were scared.

"I suppose I've done you a disservice, daughter." Rebekah's voice was stilted and formal. "And for that, I am sorry. I shouldn't have shielded you. It's just—" She trailed off. When she started talking again, it was so low Hannah could barely hear her. "Slavery, it's so ugly. What it does to people. What it turns them into. Both the masters and the slaves. I didn't want you to witness that ugliness. To be affected by it." She sighed. "But you're right, Aaron, you've been right all along. This *is* part of her world, however ugly and cruel it is, and she needs to understand it. Maybe this way, teaching for Harry, Hannah can begin to understand. I would rather he teach her than anyone else."

Rebekah grew silent, still facing away from them, looking off into their smallish yard, into the gloaming. "Justice, *Tzedek*, it's our way. It always has been."

Hannah could hardly breathe. She clenched her hands in between her legs. "Does that mean . . . I can?" She could barely finish her question.

Rebekah pressed her lips. "Yes, but—" Before Rebekah could finish Hannah was in her arms, squeaking and hopping up and down.

"But, child. Stop that and listen." Hannah stopped jumping, but she couldn't stop grinning, and she swung her arms back and forth with pent-up energy.

"Child," Rebekah said with gravity, placing a palm on each of her daughter's cheeks. "If anything gets worse or the situation becomes dangerous, the arrangement ends. Do you understand?"

"Oh, thank you. Mama!" She danced around as her mother tried to hold her at arm's length. "Thank you, thank you!" Then she was twirling out of mother's embrace, skipping over to Uncle Aaron to give him a kiss on the cheek. "Thank you both!"

Aaron spoke, flushed with pleasure. "But if one spark drops near that powder keg, Hannah, you're finished there. I hope you understand that."

Hannah nodded, ecstatic. "I understand."

Rebekah looked at Hannah, but she spoke to Aaron. "If a spark drops, it will already be too late."

CHAPTER 7

Per Harry's instructions, Hannah was to arrive at his school at ten each morning and teach Bintu for two hours until just after the noon hour. She would then help Bintu and Harry feed all the young students a large midday meal before their long treks back to the rice or indigo plantations outside of town, and then she would go back to Cardozo's Dry Goods and work in the store for her mother. Instead of being tutored, for the next three weeks Hannah would *be* the tutor, and so her mother considered her educational needs covered for the time being. All thanks to her uncle and the magic word—*Tzedek*.

Her first day at school was the following Monday, and the days between when her mother agreed and that first morning dragged longer than any days in Hannah's life. When she woke up on Monday, way too early judging from the purple shadows outside her window, she practically sprung from her bed like a coil, and was dressed and ready to go hours before ten.

Her mother chuckled at her, but in a kindly way.

"*Gatinha*, I don't think I've ever seen you so nervous. Jumpy like a young colt." Rebekah smoothed her daughter's wild curls back from her forehead. "But it's good that you're nervous. It means you care."

As soon as she heard the church bells strike half past nine, Hannah put down the cotton she'd been shelving and trotted up to the front of the store. Her mother stood behind the counter, looking proud.

"Here," Rebekah said, and handed Hannah two hard candies and her small woven basket. "Go on, get going. You don't want to be late for your first day, do you?"

So off Hannah went, the bell over the door jingling merrily on her way out. It was an exceptionally beautiful morning in Charles Town. A light spring breeze zipped through the trees, making the Spanish moss dance under the branches, the live oaks looking like stately old ladies shaking out their skirts. Hannah skipped along with her basket in one hand. Unlike the larger, more burdensome delivery basket she usually carried, this one merely contained two cedar pencils her uncle had given her, two pieces of precious paper, a page from the *Carolina Gazette*, cornbread, and the two hard candies rolled in a bit of cloth. Hannah felt so light she could almost float away above the houses and the bright green-gold leaves.

She was surprised that the school was so close to her home, yet she'd never known it existed until mere weeks before, as it was just a few blocks before she turned onto Coming Street. When she saw the yellow house at the end of the small lane, her stomach bunched. She shifted the basket to her other hand, wiping the sweaty one on her checked dress. As the church bells from St. Michael's began to chime the tenth hour, she stepped up to the schoolhouse door. She waited until the bells stopped and then knocked sharply.

The same boy opened the door for her, again with his wide smile. "Hello, miss," he said as if he was expecting her, and stepped aside for her to enter. The bright spring sun poured through the open windows onto ten or so students clustered around the long table in the middle. Harry sat with them, showing them something on one of the slates.

"Miss Hannah, good morning. Right on time." Harry passed the slate to one of the older boys and stood. Hannah looked around, noting that there were only male students around the table. Bintu seemed to be the only girl among them. Harry beckoned for her to join him in the front of the room, and she did, nervously swinging her basket as she took her place next to him.

"Students, your attention please," Harry said in a commanding voice. Instantly all the quiet murmurings ceased, and the students kept their eyes down, peeking up at her from time to time. "This is another teacher that is going to be helping me over the next few weeks. Can you all please greet Miss Hannah? Say 'Hello Miss Hannah.'"

Harry waved his hands like an orchestra conductor as the class said in unison, "Hel-lo Miss Han-nah." The greeting ended in a ripple of giggles.

"Hello, class," Hannah responded, suddenly feeling very adult.

Harry clapped. "All right. That's all. Back to your studies."

As the children settled themselves, Harry led Hannah toward the back of the schoolhouse. "She is out here."

At the back of the school room a door opened into the kitchen yard. Although she had been out here before, with her first delivery, Hannah took better note of her surroundings now. Across the threadbare expanse of dirt, a cooking hearth consisting of stacked stones was tucked against a far, stand-alone wall with a small fire burning under a pot and a thin plume of smoke drifting into the spring sky. The structure reminded Hannah more of a shed for goats than a kitchen.

Unlike her mother's well-equipped backyard kitchen, this one had only a rickety old table with a pitcher and a basin where the children could wash their hands. A well was located at the back of the yard near the necessary.

Like everywhere else in Charles Town, the water smelled like the mud and murk of the swampy coastal land, and Hannah wrinkled her nose as a passing breeze brought the swampy stench of the privy. Sitting in a chair, facing the other direction, was Bintu. She had a pile of peas in the lap of her apron, and she was shelling them into a bowl nestled against her stomach. Each handful of peas hit the bowl with a sound like a muffled rain burst. When Bintu saw Hannah and Harry step outside, she stood, scooping the pile of unshelled peas from her apron onto the wooden table, being careful not to dump them on the ground. She placed the wooden bowl to the side of the pile of peas before joining Harry and Hannah.

"Bintu," Harry said. "This is Miss Hannah, your new teacher."

Bintu looked up at Harry with confusion. When her expression cleared, it settled into a stony mask. Hannah felt nervous. Bintu had seemed friendly to Hannah on her previous visit, but today her face was frigid, like petrified wood. She seemed a different girl than the one who had greeted Hannah before.

"Teacher," Harry said. "Miss Hannah is your teacher." He nodded at Bintu.

"Teacher Hannah," she repeated.

"Hello," Hannah said.

"Why don't you two work out here?" Harry said. "And maybe you could help Bintu with the midday cooking."

"Absolutely, Mister Harry." Hannah's insides were squirming. She desperately did not want Harry to go back inside and leave her alone to *work* with Bintu, whatever that meant. "Um, Mister Harry?"

The man stopped on the step leading up to the doorway and looked over his shoulder at her. "Just Harry, if you please, Miss Hannah."

"Hannah is fine for me too," she said. "But, Harry. What should I do? How do I teach her?"

A warm smile emerged as Harry came back down the steps. "It's all right, Miss Hannah. You'll do just fine." He led her over to two cane back chairs sitting in the shade of a massive pecan tree and gestured for Bintu to join them. The two girls sat side by side.

"Bintu here is very clever, as I think I've mentioned."

Bintu watched Harry's mouth intently.

"She's also a trifle . . . well, I suppose homesick would be one word for it." Harry looked at Bintu with a soft sympathy, eyes bright with what might've been tears, or could've been anger. "It's not easy for any of us, when they take us, and the passage, and then everything is so new and so bloody horrible." He shook his head. "Your job is very simple, Miss Hannah. Talk to Bintu. Talk to her a lot. Instruct her to do things with you, take care of the garden or sewing, for instance. She's mad for sewing, as you can see."

Sure enough, Bintu had produced a strip of cloth from beneath her skirt, and was embroidering it while Harry spoke.

"And while you're doing those tasks, hoeing the garden or making preserves or doing the laundry, talk to her. Tell her what you're doing, or about your family and homelife. It doesn't matter what it's about. Bintu needs to learn English as fast as she can, and the best way to do that is to hear it and use it. She's been able to absorb some, on the trip here, but she needs help. Your help."

The cold sweat on Hannah's brow was drying in the spring breeze. Harry's calm words of instruction gave her confidence. *I can do this.* She could certainly talk to Bintu, even if the girl wouldn't answer.

"Sometimes you'll need to help her out, like with her name. For those moments, you should use this." Harry went into the schoolhouse, reappearing a moment later with slate and chalk in hand and handing them both to Hannah. "When you need to, write something down. But remember, you're not here to teach her how to write; that's forbidden. Only how to understand and speak passable English, and then to read, eventually."

Bintu remained bent over her sewing. The needle glinted in and out of the cloth with amazing speed. Hannah thought Bintu might even be faster than her mother, and that was saying something. Harry gave Hannah one last encouraging glance, and then returned to his classroom.

Bintu and Hannah sat in silence for many minutes. Bintu continued sewing, not looking up. The only thing moving was the breeze in their skirts and Bintu's hands. Hannah listened to the wind in the fluttery pecan leaves and the birdsong with the slate and chalk in her lap, admiring the intricate designs Bintu had sewn into her dress. In stripes and whorls, diamonds and swirls, Bintu had transformed the poor-quality sackcloth into something exquisite.

It was only when Hannah tried to get her attention that she realized that Bintu did not know that she had a new name. Harry had told her that Bintu had been renamed Chastity by her new master and mistress, the Reverend and Mistress Harte. But the girl did not seem to know that she was now Chastity and not Bintu.

"Chastity?" Hannah said over the girl's bowed head. The girl didn't respond; she didn't even twitch. "Bintu?"

The girl's head jerked up and she regarded Hannah warily for a moment. But at least she was now engaged. And Hannah had a clear path before her. *The first thing I have to do is teach Bintu her new name.*

Hannah decided to use the slate and chalk for this task and wrote out her own name in the loopy script her mother had taught her. When she'd finished, she held it up so Bintu could clearly see it and then, while drawing a line beneath it as she spoke, said, "Hannah." She pointed at herself and then looked at Bintu expectantly.

Bintu waited a few seconds, eyes darting back and forth from Hannah's face to the slate. Finally she said, "Hannah," and pointed at Hannah. Hannah beamed at her. Bintu's face wore the same stony expression of distrust. No matter, Hannah plunged ahead.

Hannah used part of her apron to wipe away her own name. Now she wrote *Bintu* in script across the slate, hoping she was spelling it right. She held it up, pointed at Bintu, and said, "Bintu."

Recognition sparked in Bintu's eyes. "Bintu," she said easily, pointing at herself.

Can she read? Hannah wondered. Here came the hard part. How to tell the girl that she had been renamed. Given a slave name? How could she possibly understand that?

Hannah used her apron to wipe away the name again, and in its place, she wrote, *Chastity.* Pointing out each syllable as she went, Hannah pronounced, "Chas-ti-ty." And then she jabbed a finger at Bintu, who cringed. Hannah nodded and tried to smile, but it didn't quite come off. "Chastity," she repeated, and pointed again at the girl.

With reluctance, Bintu repeated the name, "Chastity," and then pointed at herself. Understanding flooded her features, and the look she gave Hannah was very lonely and very old. "Chastity," she whispered.

Hannah lowered the slate to her lap, sympathy for the lost girl welling up her throat. She dug into the basket and handed Bintu the candy her mother had given her that morning. It seemed like a paltry offering, but Hannah wanted to offer her something. Bintu took the piece of hard brown sugar and bobbed her head in thanks, but then she just stared at it, as if wondering what to do. Hannah took her own piece of candy, showed it to Bintu, and popped it into her mouth.

Bintu looked at her with amazement, and then tentatively stuck out the tip of her tongue and brought the candy to it. Her eyes suddenly widened and her eyebrows jumped up her forehead. She popped it into her mouth as if scared Hannah would take it back. The sadness melted partly away from the young girl's expression as she enjoyed what might have been her first piece of candy.

"Candy," Hannah told her around her own mouthful of hard sweetness.

Bintu studied Hannah. It was hard not to think of some predatory bird when looking at the girl's eyes; they were so striking, so piercing, and very, very wary.

"Candy," Hannah said again, and took her candy out of her mouth to show to Bintu.

"Can-dee," the other girl said.

"Yum," Hannah replied, popping the treat back in her mouth.

"Yum," Bintu agreed.

And just like that, Hannah decided that she would not, under any circumstances, teach Bintu using her slave name. She was Bintu, and that was that. Here, at least, she would not be Chastity. Here Bintu could be herself, with her own name.

CHAPTER 8

Hannah would arrive each day and greet Harry and the boys, who would invariably be chanting or singing or repeating a Bible passage, trying to get their letters down, and then she would smile and join Bintu in the backyard kitchen.

As the only girl in the school, most, if not all, of the household chores fell to Bintu. Hannah thought she must be glad for the help of preparing the large midday meal that fed the two of them, Harry, and, most importantly, a gaggle of growing, underfed boys. Bintu was unsure about some of the ingredients, kitchen tools, and methods of cooking, so Hannah found that through the preparation of the midday meal, the girls could find plenty of things to talk about. Or rather, Hannah could always find something to talk to Bintu about, even if Bintu didn't respond.

Although initially reluctant to open up to Hannah, Bintu softened a bit more each day. It didn't seem that she was an unkind person, just that her recent experiences had made her distrustful of, well, everyone. Truthfully, Hannah couldn't blame her. She wanted to ask

Bintu about what had happened to her, but the language impediment made such a complex question beyond reach.

With cooking and household chores taking up their hands, conversation was easy although a bit one-sided. At first, Hannah named everything she could see, holding the object of consideration up as she intoned the nouns. Some things, Hannah labeled, making a little tag tied on to the object with a string so that Bintu could practice reading as well as speaking.

"Spoon . . . pot . . . peel . . . " Hannah would say as she and Bintu wandered around their small kitchen, touching objects as they went, whispering their names back to them like an incantation. "Onion . . . potato . . . beans . . . cucumbers . . . "

Harry was right, Bintu was an incredibly fast learner. It wasn't just that she was smart, but she understood *how* to learn, that the repetition of the name plus the tactile experience of touching the item was a crucial and vivid piece of the puzzle.

Within the first week, Hannah had taught Bintu some basic word combinations that would help her with everyday living and interactions. Phrases like, "How are you?" and "What is your name?" and, of course, "Yes, Master" and "Yes, Mistress." Hannah made sure to teach Bintu the correct forms of address for the Reverend and Mistress Harte. To call them by the wrong name would be a misery to everyone except the Hartes, who would take pleasure in punishing such an infraction. Hannah got the sense, from talk in the store and snippets overheard from Uncle Aaron's and her mother's conversations, that Reverend Harte had purchased Bintu because of her looks as much as for her capacity for labor.

It wasn't just tilling, hoeing, stirring, and repeating words; the girls had some genuine moments where they could be just girls together. One morning, as they were putting together a cold lunch, Hannah was slicing hard yellow cheese and chopped off a piece for Bintu.

"Try this," she said, miming eating with her hand.

Bintu popped the cheese into her mouth. A grin slowly formed as she chewed. She expressed her delight with one of her favorite new words, "Yum."

A little later, Hannah straightened up from the hearth to find Bintu carving off a hunk of butter. Before Hannah could say a word, Bintu popped the slab into her mouth. A look of dismay instantly registered as she shook her head. "No," she said through a mouthful of butter. "No yum."

What made the biggest impression on Bintu in the first few weeks wasn't Hannah, or the words she was teaching Bintu, but King Sol. The raggedy old fighting tom had taken to following his young mistress to her place of industry, and regularly made the trek to and from Harry's school with Hannah. He didn't really walk with her, per say, but would stay abreast of her for a few supple strides, then leap a fence and disappear between two buildings, only to reappear, sitting stately, on a fence post a few houses down, cleaning a paw on his perch. From what Hannah could gather from Bintu's expressions of delight the first time Sol had rounded a corner of the schoolhouse and stalked his way into their garden, Bintu had never seen a domesticated feline before, at least not one like King Sol.

She seemed especially taken with his eyes, repeatedly pointing at Sol's big orange, lantern-like eyes and then to her own. "Like mine," she'd say.

"Yours are blue," Hannah corrected. "You have blue eyes, Bintu."

"Blue eyes," Bintu repeated.

As the days passed and Bintu's progression with language grew, Hannah learned more about Bintu's life at the Hartes' as well. She spoke, haltingly at first, then with more confidence, about the other people she lived and worked with—Malachi, a young boy, and Nan, the cook—all three sleeping in a hot attic space.

"Nan," Bintu had informed her, "makes noise when she sleep," illustrating her point with garish snorts and snores.

Bintu didn't seem particularly open about life with the Hartes. If Hannah asked her anything too specific, her face would close up like a door slamming, and she would remain silent. Apparently, there was a grey cat at the house that was a nuisance to everyone in the household, hiding under furniture and swiping at passing ankles, especially Bintu's. Hannah saw the red gashes the cat had left on her ankles.

Bintu adored King Sol and he reciprocated, pouring all of his stately tomcat meows toward the back door when they arrived until Bintu threw it open and said, "Good morning!" to sometimes both of them and sometimes, Hannah swore, only to King Sol. The old tabby's absolute devotion grew as the days passed, the cat making his affection obvious with head butting and slow, sultry blinks whenever Bintu was about.

"He has a good name," Bintu remarked over his rusty purr one afternoon as they were taking a break. Bintu was petting the surprising zigzag of bright sunflower yellow on King Solomon's forehead, or whatever the cat equivalent of that was. "He is like royalty, like king."

King Sol, sprawling in a shaft of sunlight, flipped over and revealed his ragtag belly, making Bintu and Hannah laugh.

"Oh yes," Hannah said in mock formality. "So regal."

Grinning from ear to ear, Bintu popped up and sprang a surprisingly suitable curtsey. "Majesty," she said to the cat, and held that ridiculous pose for a moment until Hannah heard a snuffle escape the rim of Bintu's bonnet, which set them both off into gales of laughter.

This became Hannah's new life, a life she grew to love and anticipate each day. Every morning, she would get up earlier than usual, set to her customary chores, make sure her mother was prepared for the day, and head for Harry's, usually accompanied by King Sol. She felt in-charge, competent, and so grown-up as she strode through the streets of her small, growing town, King Sol lagging a few steps behind and looking thoroughly uninterested, but following her just the same.

When she arrived at school, she and Bintu would set to the daily tasks and begin to prepare the midday meal, chattering like a pair of tufted titmice. At first, it was only Hannah's voice that made the verbal melody, but soon enough Bintu had enough words at her disposal to join in, making their exchanges and work together more fun.

Bintu and Hannah were soon speaking to one another about more complicated matters. It went beyond the naming of objects and defining of verbs. Soon Hannah was telling Bintu her life story, and her mother's stories too. Bintu would ask questions and remember the stories later on.

Bintu even began to use some of Hannah's mother's choice phrases, which Bintu said in a perfect rendition of Rebekah's voice, even though they'd never met. Hannah had more than once heard a thump or crash and then, almost eerily, her mother's "Oh dear!" in Bintu's voice.

Bintu and Hannah had moments at the head of the class as well, when Harry was otherwise occupied. There, she and Bintu would confer about a particular word, and, once decided, Hannah would write out each letter on a slate, one by one, until one of the boys guessed it.

The girls realized one fateful morning that certain words would, to put it mildly, set the boys off if they were in a particular mood. In fact, it only took one of them to be in such a mood. When one started up, the rest of the class usually joined in soon afterward.

One morning, Bintu had whispered, "Pickle," in Hannah's ear. As soon as all the letters were ranged out on slates, one brave student, Ben, tried to sound them out, as he switched from foot to foot.

"Pick—" he said with confidence, then his face scrunched up. "Pick . . . leigh?"

One of the boys behind him snorted.

"Pickley?" he tried again. This time there were two more muffled chuckles.

A high clear voice sliced through the air. "Pickle!" Sukey said shrilly, holding the table with both hands. "It says pickle!" And he beamed so wide his face looked as if it might crack.

Sukey's air of jubilant triumph for guessing the ridiculous word struck the entire class as hysterical, and they simultaneously burst into laughter. Bintu and Hannah could only manage to maintain their teacherly silence for a few moments before joining in.

The morning of the last day of her first week, as Hannah was preparing to leave her house, King Sol making himself a nuisance around her ankles, warbling in his scratchy cat's voice, her mother set down a small bundle wrapped in a scrap of muslin next to Hannah's basket.

"What's this?" Hannah asked, picking it up to look at it closely. Her mother had folded the muslin so that if Hannah wanted to pry into it, she'd have a hard time unwrapping the expertly tied cloth.

"Never you mind." Rebekah whisked the tightly tied bundle out of Hannah's hands and deposited it in her basket. "You give that to your student when you get to the school." Rebekah took over the tying of Hannah's bonnet and wouldn't meet her daughter's eyes. She never referred to Bintu by her real name, nor did she utter her slave name. She just called her "the girl" or "your student."

"You . . . you got her a gift?"

Rebekah finished her quick bow under the girl's chin. "Not really a gift, just an offering, from one seamstress to another."

When she'd gotten back to the store the day before, Hannah had told her mother that Bintu was an especially adroit sewer, and Rebekah's thick dark brows had tweaked in an interested way, but she'd said nothing. Now Hannah understood.

Rebekah handed her the basket and swatted her on the hip to move her toward the door.

"You don't want to be late, *gatinha*, do you? Off you go!"

And just like that Hannah found herself on the front stoop of Cardozo's, bell tinkling as the door swung shut behind her.

When Hannah got to the school, the boys were clustered around Harry, who gave Hannah a wave and continued with his lesson. He pointed at a chalk *A* on the slate in his hand and began, "*A* was an archer," he started, and the boys immediately chimed in, "and shot at a frog."

Harry erased the chalk letter with his handkerchief and wrote a capital *B* on the slate. "*B* was a blindman . . . "

"And led by a dog," the boys finished in unison.

As Hannah reached the door to the backyard kitchen, she heard Harry start up the next verse.

"*C* was a cutpurse," he began.

"And lived in disgrace!" the boys all shouted back, louder than ever. Hannah chuckled; they loved that line.

Hannah stepped out into the dirt yard and squinted, blinking in the bright spring light. She spotted Bintu at the far edge of the kitchen garden with a wide hat on, wielding a hoe in the rows of corn. Hannah put her basket on the worktable and looked around for a hoe of her own to join Bintu in the rows.

When she stepped into the dirt bed, Bintu looked up. Every time Hannah saw Bintu's eyes was like the first time; they absolutely took her breath away. Bintu smiled.

"Hello, Miss Hannah," she said in much-improved English. "How are you today?"

Hannah smiled back, proud of her student. "I am very well, Miss Bintu, and how are you?"

"Well. Thank you, miss."

They worked companionably side by side for a few minutes, listening to a bird's intricate trills and the wind rustling the trees overhead. Sounds of a growing city—the blacksmith's clang, the clip-clop of hooves, the sawing of wood and bang of hammers—drifted from the direction of Charles Town.

When they got to the end of all four rows, Hannah blotted the sweat from her face with her apron and headed toward the shed with Bintu behind her. In the kitchen, they hung up their hoes, took off their straw hats, and fanned themselves with the wide brims, taking turns to pour from a pitcher of boiled lemon water. The lemon water was courtesy of Harry, who often managed to get lemons when they were brought from the West Indies.

Hannah wiped her mouth with her sleeve and watched as Bintu pulled a handful of potatoes from the bin under the worktable in the middle of the dirt yard, placing them on the table and reaching back under for another handful. The new potatoes were tiny, red, and plump, like radishes.

Hannah put a large pot filled with water from the pump on a grate among the hot coals of the hearth. She always made sure that the water boiled before she cooked anything to avoid sickness and fever. When she stood, she caught a glimpse of the basket and the corner of the bundle her mother had sent with her. She retrieved it and handed it to Bintu, who looked at it quizzically.

"What?" she said, which was their shorthand for anything Bintu wanted to know about.

Hannah shrugged. "I don't know what. It's a gift, from my mother."

Bintu frowned and shook her head. She didn't understand that the package was a gift for *her*.

"Here," Hannah handed the package to her more firmly, urging the girl to take it.

Bintu reached out and took it, although she still seemed unsure. She unwrapped the muslin to reveal needles, thread, and brightly colored swaths of cloth. On top of it all was a small piece of intricate lace. Bintu gasped and pressed her fingers to her mouth. She held the lace up to the strong sunlight, admiring it as the light lit it up like a piece of glowing cobweb.

"Who?" she asked.

"My mother. She's the one who gave it to you. Mo-ther." Hannah pressed her hand over her heart as she said this and then held her hands clasped across her body as if she was rocking an infant. When she next looked at Bintu, the girl's intense blue eyes were swimming with tears. She nodded and then looked down at her gift.

"Mother," she said, and then pressed the package, still in its muslin wrapping, to her heart. "Mother," she whispered again.

Hannah's heart clenched in her throat. *Where is Bintu's mother? What does she think has happened to her daughter?* Hannah couldn't imagine how it would feel to never see her mother again. A wave of empathy washed over her, and she tentatively reached out her hand to touch Bintu's shoulder. The girl looked up, tears streaking her cheeks, and Hannah's eyes stung.

"You miss her, don't you? Your mother?" she asked.

Bintu listened carefully, then nodded. She wiped her cheeks with the heel of her hand. "Please tell your mother thank you," she said as she refolded the sewing materials in the cloth and tucked them under her apron. "Thank you very most."

"Very much," Hannah corrected. "Thank you very much."

"Very much," Bintu whispered, and turned back to the potatoes.

CHAPTER 9

As Hannah grew closer to the boys and to Bintu, she began to observe Harry as well. She realized that Harry's Negro School was different. Children weren't his only students. Adults came at night; she'd heard the boys speak of it.

Although she had never taught anywhere else, she could tell how special this place was, and she guessed it was because of Harry.

"Are there other schools like this?" she asked him one day as they were cleaning off the slates on the back step in the early afternoon sun.

He took a long time to erase his slate. "No," he said simply, and placed it to dry in the sunlight. "There aren't many schools for slaves like this one."

"I meant, are there other schools as successful as this one," Hannah said, wiping the wet gray rag across the face of the slate.

Harry looked startled for a moment, and then flashed a rare grin, warming her like the last rays of a sunset.

But the moments she loved the very best, even more so than

those with Harry or when the boys brought her small offerings from their own tables and gardens, were her times with Bintu. The girl's language skills had surpassed Hannah's ability to teach, so now they just talked. About everything. About Bintu's life as well, her life before she'd been taken. The good things, like her grandmother's hands or her sister's lovely singing voice, and about the bad ones as well.

Hannah got the full measure of it the day Bintu showed up with her head shorn. When she first arrived, Bintu's hair had been whorls and braids, each plait making an intricate design on her scalp. A few weeks after, she'd appeared at Harry's with her hair in a French braid, and when Hannah asked her about it, Bintu set her lips and shook her head. Hannah had a feeling that her new hairdo had something to do with her mistress, Agnes Harte, but every time Hannah had asked, Bintu shut down. That braid had been long, trailing over one shoulder, and as thick as her wrist near the base of her head.

Without the braid, Hannah barely recognized her friend. She found Bintu weaving sweetgrass baskets in the shade of a magnolia tree. Hannah went to join her, and when Bintu looked up, the sight of her gave Hannah a jolt. It wasn't just her poor head, shorn to her scalp with some patches bloody and scraped, it was also the look of absolute misery in her eyes.

Hannah sat down heavily in the chair and dropped her basket by her feet.

"Bintu," she said in a small voice. "Bintu, what happened to you?"

For a while, Bintu didn't answer; she just continued to weave the basket, over under, over under. When she finally answered, it wasn't much information. "Mistress cut my hair. I broke a plate."

When Hannah followed up with, "Why?" Bintu merely shook her head and repeated herself, offering no more explanation. "Mistress cut my hair."

Hannah was flabbergasted. She had absolutely no response to an act of unprovoked barbarity. It was not in her frame of reference to understand how one human could shave another's head against her wishes, and to do it so badly as well. Probably purposefully. It dawned on Hannah, for perhaps the first time in her life, that the mistress had shorn Bintu's head for spite, to inflict as much pain as possible. But for what?

Hannah picked out some sweetgrass from the basket at Bintu's feet and began her own, observing Bintu out of the corner of her eye and feeling her scalp shiver as a rivulet of blood dribbled down from a cruel-looking abrasion to stain the girl's sackcloth collar. *Mistress must've used a very dull razor to do such a terrible job.*

There was an older scar there too. Not much older though, shiny and darker than the rest of Bintu's skin, looking like it had just recently healed. It started at the base of her skull, stretching to just over her left ear. Although Bintu's new welts looked painful and nasty, this older scar was much longer.

"And your scar? The old one? How did you get it?"

When Bintu looked up with her defeated expression, Hannah touched the place on the back of her own head where Bintu's scar now showed clearly. "How?"

Bintu nodded, pursed her lips, and resumed weaving. She said nothing, and Hannah thought she was not going to answer.

"It was a day, like this one," she began. Bintu's hands wove in rhythm with her speech, still with some awkward words and a slightly stilted cadence, but a hypnotizing rhythm all the same.

"There were many people at the river for the shrimp, that were also many," Bintu continued, intent on her weaving. "It was cool under the shade of the trees. And the canoe, this boat, it was long and filled with men, yet quiet. We had no idea it was there, until it was right there before us."

Hannah's hands stopped as she listened.

"We only knew when they attacked. We never heard them until they were on us." Bintu's eyes were unfocused and troubled, their bright blue dimming into the hue of a stormy sea. "They had clubs.

I was one of the first to get—" Bintu trailed off, putting her hand to the back of her head. "I never even saw who. When I woke, I was at the bottom of a canoe, tied, and there were drums beating all around me. A big man sat on a chair, like a throne, in the middle. I could see the back of it where I lay with the others."

"The others?"

"Other slaves," she clarified.

The words hung in the air between them; Hannah had never heard Bintu refer to herself as a slave, just as Hannah never called her Chastity, although Harry did at times. It was a topic the girls avoided.

Bintu met Hannah's gaze. "I sat up, even though I was very dizzy. I was hurt. Here," she pointed at the back of her head. "I sat up and I saw the last edges of my land slip away. Then I knew I would never see my family again. The slavers had gotten me. My head hurt so much, and I wanted to lie down to sleep again, but I had to see. Because it was the last time I would see my homeland."

Bintu stopped talking and the two sat in silence as Bintu's hands worked tirelessly on her basket.

"Everywhere on the slavers' boat, people swayed to the drums. It was the worst day of my life, and they were smiling. And that was only the beginning of a very bad dream; what do you call it?"

"Nightmare," Hannah whispered, her tongue a stone in her throat.

"Yes, a nightmare." Bintu nodded, looking at the almost-finished basket in her lap. "And I can't wake up."

CHAPTER 10

It wasn't long after this that Hannah began to understand that Harry was in trouble, he just didn't know it yet. She had bits and pieces of information gleaned from a neighbor's house, around the dinner table for Shabbat, but mostly in her mother's store when she was set to task in one of the crowded aisles. People milled around—women mostly, with children in tow, or servants—and would forget she was there or not notice her altogether, speaking freely to her mother and one another behind their flapping fans and broad bonnets.

Rebekah usually had little use for the gossip mill of Charles Town, but one day in mid-July, as Hannah was in the sticky business of measuring out honeycombs, two women came in that Hannah didn't recognize. She knew most of her mother's customers by sight, but these two were unknown to her.

That Wednesday, when the bell above the store's entrance tinkled, Hannah looked up from her spot slicing and dividing the tenacious honeycombs. Her mother was folding linen halfway down the counter and, when she saw who her customers were, Rebekah straightened her spine immediately and dropped the cloth. She glanced at Hannah with a curious expression.

"You're dripping, dear," was all she said before she hurried toward the pair, skirts rustling.

Hannah wiped the rim of the bowl she was working out of and used a knife to cut another section of the honeycomb, translucent with honey, all the while watching the new customers out of the corner of her eye.

The two women were about her mother's age and well dressed. From years at her mother's knee and in the store handling all sorts of cloth, Hannah could tell that these were wealthy ladies. Not as wealthy as Mistress Pinckney with her satiny blue gowns, but wealthy enough. Their hair curled into ringlets where it escaped from their leghorn straw bonnets. Their cotton dresses were of the highest order with tucks and bows on the bodice, three-quarter length sleeves with lace on the hems, and tiny pink roses embroidered on the skirt. Outfits altogether too fancy for a simple shopping trip on a Wednesday morning. Something told Hannah that these ladies weren't here for the dry goods.

Rebekah greeted the two with her back to Hannah, so Hannah couldn't see her expression. The ladies smiled with curled lips and moved a little into the store—not quite to the counter, but almost. One of them carried a basket that Hannah instantly recognized as her own. It was one of theirs from the store, but it had gone missing. Hannah thought she'd left it at school and planned to retrieve it when she was there next. But now, here it was, with this strange lady in the too-fancy skirt bristling with tiny pink roses.

Hannah was, to put it mildly, confused. How did this woman, who looked as if she was smelling a particularly hot necessary, get her basket?

The women spoke in murmurs, too low for Hannah to hear, and a tendril of alarm bored its way into Hannah's heart. The taller one with the roses on her skirt and the pale curled tendrils framing her face handed the basket back to Rebekah. When she caught sight of Hannah in the gloomy back of the store, she frowned sharply and murmured something to her compatriot. The other one, with watered-down red hair, looked at Hannah with similarly hateful eyes. Hannah felt a little queasy. *What do the two ladies want with me? And why are they acting like they hate me?* Rebekah caught Hannah's eye and, ever so slightly, shook her head, which only served to confuse Hannah even more. *What did I do wrong?*

"Ladies," Rebekah said as she reached forward to gently grasp the taller woman's elbow. "Won't you come upstairs to my parlor and join me for some tea?"

The tall woman inclined her head, and Rebekah led them toward the door in the back of the store. As they passed her workstation, Rebekah introduced them.

"Mistress Harte, Mistress Atkins, this is my daughter, Hannah." Hannah lowered her eyes and popped a curtsy, her hands hovering an inch or two above her skirt to avoid getting honey all over her apron. She tried to keep her eyes glued to her glistening hands, but her heart had jumped to a triple beat. Had her mother said Mistress Harte? The one who had shorn Bintu's head?

"Hannah, Mistress Harte is the Reverend Harte's wife, and is very active in her church." Rebekah's eyes were trying to tell Hannah something, but Hannah couldn't understand what. "And this is Mistress Atkins, secretary for the vestry. They've come to return your basket."

"Pleased to meet you, Mistress Harte, Mistress Atkins. Thank you for returning my basket. Wherever did you find it, and how on earth did you know it was mine?" Hannah asked in her most polite, talking-to-grown-ups voice.

When Mistress Harte spoke, it was like the first hard frost of the season. "We found it at Harry's Negro School when we went for our monthly evaluation of the slave children's progress. When I asked Harry, he informed me that it was yours."

Hannah didn't know why, but Rebekah looked extremely uncomfortable, twisting a swath of her apron mercilessly and glancing from the ladies to Hannah and back again.

"Ladies, please, let me offer you some—"

"I was surprised when Harry told me you were teaching there," Mistress Harte interrupted Rebekah, astonishing Hannah. "Young, proper girls, even Jewish girls, do not mingle with slave children, much less teach them anything. It is against the law, did you know that, Hannah? And the punishments are severe."

No one spoke. Hannah could feel her mother's rigid presence stir just behind her. Rebekah pushed past Hannah and inserted herself between her daughter and the two women as a fierce blush lit Hannah's cheeks. *Are these women here to punish me?* Hannah wondered. *Will they forbid me from going to Harry's?*

Rebekah stood before the haughty pair, waves of heat rippling out from her. When she spoke, her voice was all firmness and propriety. "Ladies, I must insist. Join me in my parlor. A much more appropriate setting."

Mistress Harte seemed unperturbed as she let herself be led down the narrow aisle, her bulbous skirt brushing the bags and boxes piled on the shelves. "I merely thought, Rebekah," she added in a simpering tone as they made their way, "that if *you* were unable to educate your daughter about such matters, *I* should be the one to do it."

Mistress Atkins threw a triumphant look at Hannah before she pushed her way through the narrow doorway in back, and then the door snicked shut behind them, leaving a bewildered Hannah alone in an empty store with honey all over her hands.

Rebekah didn't say much over dinner after she had spent the afternoon with the Mistresses Harte and Atkins. The Levinson twins were once again at their table, so Hannah couldn't broach the subject of the two ladies' visit with her mother as she juggled dishes and the four-year-olds' wishes. And the goblins were particularly demanding tonight, making it so Rebekah had barely a moment to sit and eat a mouthful before they had her up and running after them again. After dinner the weight of the evening chores fell to Hannah, as Rebekah walked the boys back to their (hopefully rested) mother and newborn sister.

Hannah had just finished sweeping when Rebekah came back. One look at her mother's dark countenance strangled Hannah's falsely cheerful greeting in her throat. She ducked her head, training her eyes on the dust pile she'd been trying to move toward the hearth.

Dread filled her as her mother quickly crossed the dirt floor of the kitchen house and gripped her elbow. *Something's definitely wrong.* When Hannah's eyes reached her mother's face, a weight plummeted into Hannah's stomach. Her mother was crying. It was terrifying.

"Mama!" Hannah exclaimed. "Mother, what is it? Are you all right? Are you ill?"

Rebekah shook her wet curls, seeming to realize what she was about, and took off the cloak. "I'm fine, I'm fine." After she hung up her cloak, Rebekah stood by the threshold, leaning against it.

"Mother," Hannah mewled.

"Really, *gatinha*. I am fine." She returned to Hannah's side and took her by the wrist, leading her to two cane chairs sitting by the open side of the kitchen. "But we have to talk."

Hannah sat at her mother's bidding. The icy grip of Rebekah's hand burned through the thin fabric of Hannah's sleeve.

"Those two ladies that came to visit us this afternoon, what did you make of them, Hannah?" Rebekah's gaze was red-rimmed, but gentle.

Hannah's mind went back to the afternoon, to the mix of rustling skirts, the sweet round smell of honey, and the curdling of confusion and anxiety in the pit of her stomach as those ladies in their fancy dresses interrupted her mother to talk down to her.

"To tell you truly, Mother, I didn't like them much. Not even a little." Hannah hung her head, unused to speaking out about adults, especially in front of her mother.

"Can you tell me why?" Rebekah put one cool finger under Hannah's chin, tipping it up so Hannah had to meet her eyes. "Do not worry, child, you shan't be punished for anything you say to me."

Hannah took a breath, and when she started to speak it all tumbled out. "They came in here with *my* basket and immediately acted like they hated me! They don't even *know* me! And the way they talked to you, then they said that stuff about Harry's school—" Hannah stopped, out of breath.

Rebekah nodded. "They made me angry too. Not just what they said, but how they treated you. They should have never—" Hannah felt so acutely embarrassed she tried to lower her head and study her feet, cheeks on fire. Her mother wouldn't let her drop her chin and wouldn't break her gaze. "Listen to me, Hannah. No one should *ever* make you feel ashamed of who you are, no matter who they are. Never!"

Hannah nodded, her stomach still swirling with anxiety. Those ladies in their fancy clothes with their mean, rat faces and cold eyes. She hated them so much, and her hate sickened her.

"It's not just the basket. We have another problem with the mistresses," sighed Rebekah.

"What's that?"

"They saw you there, and now they're talking. To their husbands."

Hannah felt immediate foreboding like a punch to the gut. "What are they talking to their husbands about?"

"About Harry's school. How they don't approve of it. And that they want to shut it down."

More weight dropped into Hannah's stomach.

"They don't have much power," Rebekah continued. "But their husbands do, quite a bit of it, I'm afraid. They can close down anything they want to in this town."

"I don't understand, Mother. Why would they close Harry's school?"

"It's complicated. That school is special, as is Harry. You see, when the school was started, it was in spite of the law. The law forbade anyone from educating slaves. But the SPG thought that it was important to educate slaves because they would be better workers as well as being Christians." Rebekah paused, looking thoughtfully at her daughter. "Harry was just a boy a little older than you when the school started. He was bought so that he could teach there for the parish. This was twenty years ago, before you were born. Harry has made that school what it is. Some think that Harry has taught almost a thousand slaves to read the Bible."

Hannah's eyes widened. "Amazing," she whispered as she tried to imagine a thousand students revolving through Harry's small, scuffed classroom.

"But Harry's success is the very thing that makes people afraid, and they do terrible things when they're afraid."

"Why are they afraid of Harry's school?"

"Because he's educating slaves. The people that live here are afraid of educated negroes because they think that, as soon as slaves learn how to read or write, they'll rise up against their masters. It'll be another Stono Rebellion, and men and women will be killed on both sides. Children too. That's what they think, and they might be right or they might be wrong, but they'll do anything in their powers to avoid that outcome." Rebekah leaned back, strong black eyebrows like bat wings over her eyes.

Sitting in her cane chair, spine straight, Hannah could barely believe it. Her mother was talking to her as if she were an adult, a full-grown woman in her own right. "A Jewish girl in a slave school is *not* something those women would forget. Or approve of," Rebekah continued as her countenance clouded over again. "Now they are poking around to see who else in our community might be supporting the school. They call their snooping 'looking after a young girl's virtue.' Can you believe that?" Rebekah scoffed deep in her throat. "They said that to my face, about you, my daughter, in my own parlor." She made the derisive sound again. "And they're not looking to your virtue, are they? That's not really what they're doing, is it? No, this is much more devious and serious."

"But they—"

"They have wanted an excuse to shut that school down for some time now. And then they found your basket. Now you're the excuse. Simple as that."

Hannah couldn't respond.

All the words in the world could not make this right. They were going to shutter Harry's school, and it was all her fault.

CHAPTER 11

When it was time for her next visit to the school, Hannah was worried about how she would act around Harry and Bintu now that she knew the school was in peril. *Does Harry hate me now? Does Bintu? Do they know what I've done? I didn't mean to leave my basket. Why did I forget my basket? How could I be so daft?*

It was astonishing how such a tiny thing could derail a whole school. She could barely consider what would happen to the boys, as she'd come to think of the younger students. *Where will they go if the school shuts down? Who will teach them to read? Will they just go back to the fields?* She could hardly stand it.

Hannah had one terrible night of restless sleep, tossing and turning her overheated body in the twisted sheets. Every position felt uncomfortable—the pillow too lumpy, the sheets too coarse. The weather outside matched her confusion. Heat lightning forked down every few moments, accompanied by the rumble of thunder minutes later, but the rain did not come and so the heat would not break.

The next morning at dawn, Hannah rose from her rumpled bed, finally mustering the will to get up and wash her face. As she leaned over the bucket they used as a basin, her hands felt too heavy to even wash the sleep from her eyes. Her chin drooped and she gave into the movement, dunking her head in the bucket. It fit neatly inside, only sloshing a little water out, and for one blessed moment, the noise and bustle and beehive buzz of her brain ceased to matter, and all was watery silence. *What I would give to be a mermaid,* she thought in those few stolen moments.

She withdrew her head from its wood-and-water helmet with some care and gasped.

After she'd wiped her eyes free of water, she found her mother in the doorway. Hannah was able to register the look of annoyance—probably at Hannah's lateness––turning to concern, and then the floorboards went all wobbly on her. Or was it her vision? The result was the same. She sat down hard on her tailbone.

"*Gatinha*! Are you all right? You look terrible!"

Hannah groaned. Her mother was at her side in an instant, helping her to her feet and down the narrow stairway. Rebekah helped Hannah down the hallway and she collapsed into her mother's bed; the cool back of her mother's hand on her forehead was a balm against the bonfire raging there.

"I couldn't sleep," Hannah croaked, her throat shredding at every word.

"Oh dear," Rebekah was at the basin, dunking a cloth into it and bustling back over to lay it on Hannah's forehead. "I think you have a touch of something. Here." Rebekah pulled the crumpled sheets up over her and Hannah made no protest, she just lay back and listened to the throbbing in her brain. "Let me get some Bateman's Elixir to bring your fever down."

Hannah nodded listlessly. The last thing she saw before her eyes closed was her mother rushing out the door. Then the floorboards did their thing and tilted up at her again.

The next time Hannah awoke, her mother was at her bedside with a tray, and she was shaking her shoulder.

"Hannah, wake up."

Hannah wanted to burrow back under the sweaty, overheated layers of her bed clothes and sleep more. The shaking became adamant.

"No, Hannah, wake up!"

Hannah groaned, the pounding in her head ratcheting up as she tried to open her sticky eyes. When she finally was able to unstick them, the midday brightness branded her poor swollen brain.

"Here, take this."

Hannah squinted at a spoon hovering in front of her and opened her mouth like a baby bird. In went the spoon and a sickly, sweet syrup was poured in. It smelled like the dregs of wine that were sometimes left in the cups after seder. Hannah made another sound, this one of disgust, and Rebekah gripped the girl's chin.

"Hannah, swallow. We need to get your fever down. This will make you feel more like yourself."

Hannah grimaced and swallowed, and the syrup slid down her throat, coating it in a not-unpleasant manner as it went down. Her eyes fluttered shut and she felt fevered sleep overtaking her. She hoped her mother was right, that the smelly sweet syrup would make her feel like herself again.

The next few days were a blur of heat, brightness, headaches, and sweaty sheets. The medicine did lower her fever, but it also made her feel as if she was wrapped in linen. She couldn't quite get a hold of herself—whatever *herself* was would slip out of her grip and she would be unmoored once again. She would often awaken to the spoon in front of her face and then the dark, pungent liquid was poured down her throat and she'd inevitably drift off again.

After a while, Hannah had no idea how long, except that it included two instances when she awoke in the daylight, and two when she awoke in the pitch dark, she woke up more coherent than she'd been in a while. And she woke up in the middle of an argument.

This was confusing, as she couldn't understand why two people should be arguing just outside her mother's bedroom. She was considering that this was yet another syrup-induced dream when she realized that one combatant was her mother; she'd know her voice anywhere. But the other was also familiar. Heavily accented, it took Hannah's fever-addled brain to recognize that Bintu was in her house and talking with her mother.

She struggled to sit up in bed, trying to clear the cobwebs from her head. The bed frame creaked and the fierce conversation outside her door ceased. Rebekah's head poked through the threshold an instant later. "*Gatinha*! You're up! You have a visitor," she said as she pushed the door open.

Bintu stood framed in the doorway in the sackcloth dress, straw hat, and basket in hand.

"Hello, Miss Hannah," Bintu said smoothly, smiling as she moved to her friend's bedside.

"Bintu!" Hannah croaked, and then fell into a coughing fit.

Bintu sat on the stool and took Hannah's hand, putting two fingers to Hannah's wrist and holding them there. She felt Hannah's forehead and half-turned to Rebekah. "She has a fever."

Rebekah's face had once again fallen into stern lines of disapproval. "I *know* that, child. I have been treating her and will continue to do so. See? Bateman's Elixir is just the thing for her." Rebekah took the now-familiar bottle and spoon out of her apron pocket and showed them to Bintu, who uncorked the bottle, sniffed, and grimaced.

Bintu shook her head. "No more of this medicine."

Rebekah made an exasperated noise in the back of her throat. "What in the world do you have against Bateman's? It's been doing a fine job bringing her fever down."

"No, no more of this. This is made from the seeds of poppy

flowers and the seeds are bad. They will make her feel better now but then she will stay sick." Bintu was fumbling a little for the English.

"How can you say that?" Rebekah snatched the bottle back. "How would you know?"

"I know the juice from these seeds, these flowers. Their smell." Bintu spoke in slow measured tones, choosing each word carefully. Even though Hannah's head felt as if it would pop off and roll away at any second, she felt a surge of pride for her student. "The flowers are beautiful, but the seeds have juice like milk. The juice is mixed in medicine and it is no good for any child, and especially no good for Hannah."

"Well," Rebekah said, utterly flummoxed. "It looks like my daughter did a good job of teaching you the word *no*."

"Here." Bintu reached into her basket and brought out a small bottle. "For Hannah. It will make her better, and there is no seed juice. For her . . . " Bintu searched for the word, "sick."

"Sickness," croaked Hannah, correcting her. She managed a small smile through cracked lips. "The word is *sickness*."

"For her sickness," Bintu amended.

Rebekah took the bottle and studied it. "What is it?"

"All good plants."

Rebekah took out the small stopper and smelled it. "Maidenhair, and oak bark maybe." She squinched her nose up in disbelief. "Where did you learn this? Where did you learn how to heal people with plants?"

"My mother." Bintu stood and straightened her long spine, eyes blazing. "And her mother, and her mother too. They were all *hakilimaa*. We were all wise." For a moment, Hannah could see the person Bintu would've become, tall and confident, gazing out the small window under the eaves. *Who she would've become*, Hannah amended, *if it hadn't been for that fated canoe that stole her away*. Bintu's gaze was far away for a few seconds, remembering, and then she shook her head once, sternly, bringing herself back to the present.

Rebekah's expression softened as she handed the bottle back. "So, you're an herbalist, are you?"

Bintu looked at her feet. "All the mothers in my family know these things. I learned from my mother who learned from her mother."

"Did you have your mother's eyes as well as her talent for healing?"

Bintu didn't answer this except with a very small shake of her head. "Nature has many cures. This," she held up her small blue bottle of medicine, "this is much better for a child than the juice of those seeds, Mistress Cardozo. Much better for Hannah." Bintu's hand rested on Hannah, reassuring and protective.

Rebekah cocked her head and studied Bintu. "All right. We can try it. But if she worsens, it's back to Bateman's."

"Yes, Mistress Cardozo." Bintu turned to Hannah. "Hannah, this will make you good."

"Better," Hannah corrected again. "This will make me better."

"You better hope so," Rebekah said from the doorway.

CHAPTER 12

Luckily, Bintu's remedy helped Hannah feel better almost immediately. Although it would take a few days to gain her strength back, her fever cooled and her mind cleared after a single dose. A good night's sleep and she was feeling right as rain again.

She would have moments, however—helping her mother around the shop, sweeping out the back yard, feeding the goat—when dizziness would sweep over her and she would have to pause, nauseated and breathless, and let it pass. In those moments, she often caught sight of Rebekah stilled in her own actions, looking at her daughter with concern. But Rebekah did not say anything, nor did she offer Hannah Bateman's Elixir.

When Hannah returned to Harry's school, it had been almost two weeks. As she approached the yellow school, she saw a figure come around the side of the house from the back kitchen garden. At first, she thought it was Bintu, and picked up her pace and raised a hand in greeting, but lowered it quickly. It was someone else— another slave. The woman was older than Bintu and more stooped; she bobbed her head as she passed Hannah in the drive.

Hannah was curious; there weren't many adult visitors to Harry's during daytime. Harry ran a school for adult slaves out of the classroom in the evenings so that folks could come learn after they finished their tasks. But adult slaves did not have the same sort of freedom as their children, although even those tethers were stretched tightly. So, when Hannah saw the woman exit from around back, she was a little suspicious. And when she noticed the woman tucking a blue bottle into her basket as she passed, she felt a sinking dread. It was Bintu's bottle, which did not bode well.

Hannah rounded the corner of the schoolhouse and walked through the garden gate into the back kitchen. The space had changed in two weeks; the crops were taller, especially the corn, and there was a new wooden stand next to the pump and basin. Rows of blue bottles stood on its shelves, gleaming in the sun like sapphires. Pinned to the small canopy's wooden frame were bunches of herbs, tied with twine. Bintu was beyond the row of growing corn, stooped over, harvesting something with a basket at her side.

"Hello!" Hannah said with delight, her suspicions forgotten for the moment.

Bintu straightened, her bright blue eyes finding Hannah, and waved at her, picked up her basket, and bustled over to greet her friend.

When Bintu reached her, she grabbed Hannah's hand with her free one and squeezed. Her eyes roved Hannah's face and what she saw there obviously pleased her.

"You look well," Bintu said, grinning. "I am glad."

"Me too," Hannah said. "Me too."

Hannah went inside to hang up her bonnet and greet Harry and his students. There were a few new faces in the classroom, but most of them knew Hannah. A small cheer went up from the children when they saw her, interrupting Harry in the middle of a lesson. Harry turned and smiled when he saw her.

"Miss Hannah!" he said. "We are happy to have you back. Class, can you say good morning to Miss Hannah?"

"Good morning, Miss Hannah," the class chorused.

"Good morning, class," Hannah said with the authority of a trained teacher. "I'm happy to be back, Mister Harry. Is everything all right here?"

"Never better." Harry had a finger marking his place in the Bible where he'd been reading. "Are you helping Bintu in the back garden this morning?"

"If you have nothing else pressing for me," Hannah answered. "Oh! And my mother asked me to give you this," Hannah plucked a crock of apple butter from her basket and handed it over. Harry held it up to his nose and took a deep whiff of the grainy brown condiment through the checked muslin stretched across the top.

"Please thank her, what a treat! Class, we will have some lovely apple butter for our bread today if you all do a good job learning your catechism."

Murmurs of assent filled the small room.

"All right, back to it. Thank you, Miss Hannah, and thank your mother for us. Class, can you thank Miss Hannah?"

Hannah exited the room to the jumbled chorus of, "Thank you, Miss Hannah," and peals of laughter. *The children are certainly in high spirits today,* she thought. Perhaps it was the fresh breeze after a week of sultry weather; the crisp wind off the river whisked the heat torpor from everyone's minds.

Hannah felt the same rejuvenation since she'd surfaced from her sickness. She felt almost like she'd been reborn, or sloughed off an old skin.

As Hannah approached Bintu at the long scarred wooden table, she watched her friend choose herbs from a bundle and add a pinch of this and a pinch of that to her mortar. She then lifted the kettle from off a hook, where it'd been suspended over the small fire, and poured a bit of hot water into the mix, grinding everything together with her pestle. A lovely earthy smell mixed with lavender wafted up from the greenish-brown muck at the bottom of the mortar. Hannah plunked herself down on a stool to watch her friend work.

Hannah realized that this task, which seemed wholly unrelated to school business, had to be connected to the woman she saw leaving the school on her arrival—the woman with the bottle in her basket. Curiosity overcame her as she watched Bintu strain the mixture through a piece of cheesecloth into a small ewer, and then pour this liquid into clean blue bottles. She was just about to ask when Bintu spoke first.

"Hannah," Bintu began in her strange accent. "Your mother . . . does she hate me?"

Hannah startled. "My mother? No! For what?"

"Many white women hate me. They slap me, they pinch me, they hurt me. For no reason. And I told your mother, 'No more of this medicine for Hannah.' Maybe I made her angry?"

"My mother couldn't be mad at you . . . you made me better! If she seemed angry when you visited it was because she was scared. A lot of people act angry when they're scared."

"She is scared? Of me?"

"Not of you, Bintu. She was scared to lose me. She was scared I might be taken by the sickness."

"Taken? To where? Like I was taken?"

Bintu's English had become markedly better in Hannah's absence. Bintu even seemed like a different person, more awake, more alive, more *there*.

"No," Hannah clarified. "My mother was scared I was going to die. She knows you saved me, Bintu." As always, up this close, Hannah was mesmerized by the blueness of her friend's eyes. She landed on the bird Bintu reminded her of—a kestrel, fleet and fierce. "She is grateful for what you did for me."

Bintu considered this, nodded, and kept up her grinding,

reaching a cloth-covered hand for the kettle on its long arm once again.

After a few moments of silence, Bintu spoke again. "Hannah, could you ask her something for me?"

Hannah nodded.

"The bottle, the blue one with the medicine. I need it." She waved at the rows of bottles next to her. "I only have so many, and people are asking for more."

"Yes, I'll ask her for you." Hannah hesitated, unsure whether to dive into the subject. "Bintu, you have to be careful. You're not allowed to make medicine. My mother told me, and I've heard talk in the store. You can't make tonics or anything, not for me and especially not for your own people." Hannah swallowed hard. The slave laws weren't a subject that she and Bintu broached. "It's dangerous, Bintu! Slaves aren't allowed to—"

Hannah was cut off by the jangling livery of an approaching carriage coupled with the rumbling of wheels and clip-clop of a horse. The girls looked at one another in surprise.

Carriages didn't frequent this part of town. Harry's school was tucked well away. The students, as well as Bintu and Hannah and occasionally King Sol, never arrived by carriage, but always on foot— or paw. Students, children and adults alike, living on the outer edges of Charles Town might periodically hitch a ride into town on the back of the wagon, but these rides stopped at the main square or the wharves, and they would walk the rest of the way.

Only wealthy people travelled by carriage, Hannah thought.

Bintu seemed to think the same thing because she abandoned her pestle in its mortar, and both girls lifted their skirts and ran to warn Harry.

As they reached the back door, bounding up the steps, the jangling of the reins and bits had ceased. They heard a horse whinny and snort. The visitor was on their way inside.

CHAPTER 13

Both girls tumbled through the back door and into the school room. They stood there, not knowing what to do. Harry was reading from the Bible to the fourteen students gathered around his feet, his back to the door. They couldn't yell at him to stop, could they? Should they?

Hannah lunged forward, hand at her throat, about to say something. Before she could say a word, there came a knock, but their visitor didn't wait to be admitted. The door swung open, a footman stepped out of the way, and their visitor swished into the room as Harry was intoning, "One day, after Moses had grown up, he went out to his own people and observed their hard labor . . . "

Hannah's voice caught in her throat, frozen. Mistress Harte stood listening in the doorway, the weak curls escaping her bonnet like golden lace in the sun that backlit her.

Harry, oblivious to her, went on. "Moses saw an Egyptian beating a Hebrew, one of his own people. After looking this way and that and seeing no one, he struck down the Egyptian and hid his body in the sand—"

Harry had said *Moses*, meaning he was reading from the Old Testament, and from Exodus no less. "Harry!" squeaked Hannah.

Harry stopped reading and aimed his attention to the girls in the back of the classroom. "Yes, Miss Hannah?" he said, marking his place in the Bible with a long slender finger. "What is it?"

Hannah was stupefied. All she could do was point at the doorway. "Visitor," she breathed. And Harry turned to look.

When his gaze fell on her, his face slammed shut like a trap. Hannah didn't know if it was discernible to folks who didn't know him well, but she plainly saw the light go out of his eyes and a mild mask slip over his face, disguising his features in an expression of complacency.

"Why, Mistress Harte, how lovely to see you," Harry said smoothly. "Children, please greet Mistress Harte. Her husband is Reverend Harte, a powerful man in Charles Town and one of the men who makes this school possible. Now, all together . . . "

"Hello Mistress Harte," the children chorused. The students didn't know quite what was going on, but Hannah could see by their faces that they knew it wasn't good. Sukey and Washington exchanged a guarded glance, and then their eyes drifted toward the front of the classroom, focusing on something near Harry's feet.

Mistress Harte didn't respond. She didn't even look at the boys sitting in a half circle in front of her. She walked over to Harry with ramrod-straight posture, her curls flapping by her too-sharp cheekbones. Harry watched her approach with hooded eyes and a sheepish smile.

Hannah looked for Bintu, but the girl was gone.

Mistress Harte stopped in front of Harry, still ignoring the students, and glanced down at the big black book in his hands. She was looking specifically at where his finger marked his place.

"Pray tell," she began in her grating, nasally voice, "from which book were you teaching today?"

If Harry was perturbed by her question, he didn't show it. He waited a few moments, maybe weighing whether a lie would help him, and then opened the book.

"I'm reading to them out of the Book of Exodus, Mistress Harte."

Mistress Harte took another step closer, and raised her needle-thin nose in the air, her mouth twisting in disgust and triumph. Again, Hannah was struck by the idea that Mistress Harte was constantly smelling something terrible, something rotten.

"You are fully aware, Harry, that teaching slaves *anything* but the New Testament is against the law."

"Yes, Mistress, I surely know that, but at times, we need to vary our material."

"And whoever gave you permission to do that?"

"I gave myself permission. As headmaster of this school, I am charged with teaching these young people to the best of my ability, and that's what I intend to do."

Mistress Harte's sallow face became more so, and her eyes narrowed into slits. "Scholarship aside, Harry, it is illegal to teach them out of the Old Testament, and *especially* out of Exodus." She raised one gloved hand with a delicate handkerchief to her mouth and nose. Hannah could see the small violets embroidered on it and wondered if it was Bintu who had sewn them. It looked like her handiwork.

"Surely, Mistress Harte, I could've chosen a worse passage than the one I was using? Most of Exodus does an excellent job of not only teaching literacy, but also world history. I understand that not every verse can be to everyone's liking, but if I was really trying to rile a group, I would use Galatians 5:1." He quoted, 'It is for freedom that Christ has set us free. Stand firm, then, and do not let yourselves be burdened again by a yoke of slavery.'"

Mistress Harte's eyes widened above the cloth clutched to her mouth, as if witnessing an epiphany. Hannah could hear the sharp hiss of her breath as she sucked in air, but before the woman could comment, Harry continued, his voice pouring into the air like warm amber honey.

"I can see where *some* verses from Exodus would make the staunchest slave owner uncomfortable. The Bible does say, and I quote, 'Anyone who kidnaps someone is to be put to death, whether the victim has been sold or is still in the kidnapper's possession.' As you and I both know, Mistress Harte, kidnapping is the main way that most of these people came to be in the colonies."

Hannah noticed, through her panic and hammering heartbeat, that Harry addressed her by her full title.

"But there is nothing for you to fear here, Mistress," Harry went on, "as all of these children are good Christians, having learned their catechism well. And as Luke 22:27 asks of us, 'For who is greater: the one seated at table or the one who serves? Is it not the one seated at table? I am among you as the one who serves.'"

When Harry stopped, the room became so quiet Hannah could hear a fly tapping at a window, trying to get out. *Had he really just said all that? To this woman?* Hannah wondered if Mistress Harte would scream at Harry, or strike him. After a long minute, she responded.

"Harry," she started in a clipped, low tone, having finally lowered the handkerchief from her mouth. There were odd white folds at the corners of her mouth, like scars. Her hands were by her sides, clenched into tight fists. "As you well know, conversion does not warrant emancipation. And slavery existed in Jerusalem, just as is does here."

"That may be, Mistress Harte," replied Harry in an even voice, "but since you're a learned acolyte of Christianity, you well know that Hebrew slaves were set free after seven years."

"Ridiculous," Mistress Harte sputtered. "Patently untrue. A lie."

"And I quote," Harry countered, "'When you acquire a Hebrew slave, he shall serve six years; in the seventh year he shall go free.' Quite different from our own Christian practices, don't you think, Mistress Harte?"

Outside, the birds called to one another loudly, but inside, all was hushed. Even the children were transfixed. Harry and Agnes Harte stood poised at the front of the classroom as if they were about to duel. Hannah was afraid Mistress Harte was going to hit Harry, but then the woman spun, skirt belling out around her, and strode to the door. There was a dark pink flush climbing out of her high collar and across her lower cheeks and, as she strode across the room, her heels clacked loudly on the floorboards.

At the doorway, Mistress Harte turned and jabbed a finger at Harry. "You haven't heard the end of this," she snarled. "Mark my words."

And with that, she was gone, the open door letting in a shaft of sunlight.

"I mark them, Mistress, I truly do," Harry said to the empty doorway. He stared after her, eyebrows furrowing a shelf over his eyes. When he turned back to his class, his mask had disappeared and he looked like his old self again, although more wan than normal. As he opened the book again, Hannah noticed that his hands were shaking.

"All right, boys," he said, perhaps a trifle too cheerfully, "let's continue, shall we?"

As Harry went back to reading, Hannah felt a sharp poke in her ribs. Bintu had reappeared and was looking at her with haunted eyes, hands shredding the cuff of her sack cloth sleeve.

"That's her," Bintu whispered to Hannah. "That's the one who pinches and slaps me. That is the white woman who hates me. And I belong to her. That's my mistress."

CHAPTER 14

Of course, this did not come as a surprise to Hannah, not at all. She knew Bintu had been sold to the rectory, much as Harry had been years before. But instead of being able to run a school for slave children, like Harry, who was a singular case, Bintu was relegated to the ranks of house slave in Agnes Harte's household staff.

This meant she worked in the large house's kitchens and cleaned it with a cadre of other house slaves. It also meant that she was in daily contact with Mistress Harte, and in almost daily contact with Master Reverend Harte. And it was about to be even more contact since the work at the Hartes' house required more and more of Bintu's time.

Hannah did not doubt her friend's word. Even only knowing Agnes Harte for a very short while, Hannah wouldn't put it past that woman to pinch and slap a young slave for no reason. It was, Hannah was learning, done all the time.

Certainly, Mistress Harte thought she had a good reason to take out her jealous anger on Bintu. Hannah hoped with all her heart that

Reverend Harte noticing Bintu's striking looks was not the reason behind Mistress Harte's violent dislike of the girl.

But it was more than that. Now that Hannah had her ears pricked for any news of the Harte household, it seemed that new information presented itself daily. One afternoon during a fierce rain squall when Hannah had been measuring bolts of finished cloth in the shadowy halls of the store, she'd heard a group whispering about two slaves— Daisy and Liverpool, both healer-women—who'd been burned at the stake for the crime of growing an herb garden and doling out tonics and medicines, just like Bintu was doing out of Harry's back garden.

Daisy and Liverpool were burned in the middle of Charles Town, on a green that Hannah traveled daily to get to one part of the town or another. The last whisper Hannah had heard from the other side of the shelving was, "And Jackson went the next day, and he said the coals were still glowing, and he could see bones in the ashes."

At that moment a peal of thunder had caused both to squeal and giggle shakily. There had been no more whispers of slave punishment after that.

Walking home from Harry's after the altercation with Mistress Harte, Hannah felt sick at what she'd seen. Bintu was in real trouble if her doctoring was discovered. She could suffer the same fate that had befallen many unfortunate slaves. White slave-owners were terrified that unhappy slaves would slip poison into their masters' food or drink, which wouldn't be difficult as most of those slave owners left the cooking up to their enslaved servants.

Since enslaved people outnumbered White slave owners five-to-one in this colony, there was a real terror of a slave uprising, and many cruel actions were taken to stomp out even the smallest act of rebellion. To squash that threat, Whites had decreed that slaves should not have access to anything that could be mixed up into something lethal. Slaves had limited access to doctors as well, so many of them had to do their doctoring at home, and more than a few had herbs growing to mix into tonics and potions.

The problem was, and even Hannah could see it, that Bintu seemed to have no compunction about advertising the fact that she was making these medicines. She'd told Hannah, after Mistress Harte had departed, that she'd sold out of her fever-reducing tonic the first week and had to make another, larger batch. She'd also mentioned that Harry had said something, a couple of somethings, whenever Bintu brought up her new industry. He had made it clear he opposed it.

The more people that knew Bintu was brewing concoctions from Harry's back garden, the riskier the undertaking. And this was no laughing matter. It wouldn't be a beating or a branding for Bintu if she were caught; she'd be hanged, or worse, burned at the stake, like those two poor women.

Hannah walked slowly down one dusty street after another, taking the long way home so she could sort out her thoughts. She had to convince Bintu to stop making medicines and doctoring people. Or, if that didn't work—and Hannah strongly believed it wouldn't as Bintu had a talent for the work and enjoyed helping people—Hannah had to get her out of the rectory before the Hartes discovered what she was up to and Agnes had a reason to do more than just beat the girl or cut her hair.

When Hannah returned to her family's store that afternoon, she found her mother and Uncle Aaron in a heated discussion behind the counter. They weren't speaking loudly, since a few customers still drifted up and down the aisles, but Hannah could tell from their faces that something dismal had happened. In the back of her mind, she was convinced it had to do with the incident at Harry's school. Maybe Mistress Harte had stopped by on her way back to the rectory to fill Rebekah's ear with poison.

Hannah hung her bonnet on its accustomed hook and set down her basket. She approached the pair, considering whether to ask her mother about Bintu's bottle, when her ears perked up.

"I'm telling you, it's not safe!" Aaron said. "No one is going to pay the tariffs, and the tax collector is arriving any day now! This business with the Stamp Act is making people angry. Gladstone's Sons of Liberty are protesting in the streets already. We, as a people, are in a precarious position. Don't forget that. And we both remember what happened on the banks of the Stono River. No one wants another Stono Rebellion."

Hannah stopped halfway down one aisle.

"What can we do?" Rebekah pleaded. "We can't pick up and move again. This is our home, Aaron. Our grandparents and great grandparents had to run from the Inquisition. Remember, your namesake refused to renounce his faith and they *burned* him at the stake back in Portugal. *Auto de fé.* That's why we came here in the first place—for religious freedom. We cannot run again. I'm not running again."

"I'm not saying we should run, but we need to be sensible. Your husband tasked me to look after you and your children. I gave him my word, and I will not have him return to a disaster." Aaron's hoarse whisper rose to a growl.

Rebekah pinched his sleeve. "Hush, keep your voice down!" She looked around to see if any customers had heard and caught sight of Hannah hovering at the end of the aisle. Her expression immediately changed from worry to a masked smile. "Hannah, you're home early?"

Hannah walked over to her mother and uncle, skirting the wide counter and joining them in the narrow space behind. "I am. Harry had no use for me this afternoon. Mother, what were you and Uncle Aaron talking about?"

Aaron looked at his sister, chagrined, as Rebekah searched for a response. "We were talking about things that are happening around Charles Town, politics and the like, nothing for a young, innocent girl to trouble herself with."

"I'm not that young anymore."

"And she'd not be that innocent either, after working over at the school. She sees which way the wind blows in this town, don't you, Hannah?" Aaron crossed both arms over his chest. "Do you know why the Stamp Act is causing so much trouble?"

"Well, I think so," she answered. "It's about paper, isn't it? About more tariffs, taxes to pay on every piece of paper."

"Yes, it's that and more. It's setting people up to pay more than their share, and all the profit goes back to England. That's why people are mad. And when people are mad, or scared, they do unexpected things."

"Unexpected," Hannah mused. "Like Mistress Harte's visit at school today."

"Visit?" Rebekah asked.

"She came by carriage this morning to check on the children's progress. Only it didn't go that well. She and Harry had a disagreement."

"This is what I was talking about, Rebekah," Aaron remarked. "We can't protect her over there. What was it about?"

"Mistress Harte didn't like what Harry was reading to the children. You know, from the Bible, to teach them how to read."

"What was he reading to them?" Rebekah asked. "I can't imagine that she could find fault with a lesson that came straight from the Bible. I mean, her husband's a minister and she herself is a pillar of the church."

"She didn't like that the passage was from Exodus."

This was met with silence from the adults until Uncle Aaron let out a long slow whistle.

"Exodus, the freeing of the slaves from Egypt," Rebekah breathed. "Oh my."

"You see?" Aaron said, gesturing to Hannah. "She can't continue to go there. I was all in favor of this at first, but the politics are changing. It is no longer safe, and it is not helpful that someone as powerful as Mistress Harte has noticed Hannah at Harry's. I know we were trying to broaden her horizons and show her some sense of integrity and faith, but she can't be around when that woman comes back. And that woman will be back; you can bet on it."

Hannah felt a fiery stab of anger. Uncle Aaron *wasn't* agreeing with her; he was using her own words to make her mother forbid her from helping at Harry's. And if Hannah couldn't go to Harry's, how would she know what happened to Bintu, to all of them?

"No!" Hannah burst out. "I have to go back! They're my friends!"

"No, *gatinha*," her mother said in a soothing voice, "it's not a good idea for you to be seen at Harry's school at the moment." Rebekah reached out to her daughter, but Hannah pulled away, her eyes brimming with tears of fury.

"Is that what you think or is that what Mistress Harte told you to think?" Hannah's voice broke on the last word. "What about Bintu? That woman beats her, did you know that? Slaps her, pinches her, shears her like a sheep, burns her for no reason. She leaves marks. Every day there are fresh ones."

Rebekah flinched.

"It's not fair!" she wailed. "I thought you wanted to help make things better, to make them right. *Tzedek*, and all that."

"Hannah," Aaron soothed, "it's not that easy. You can't expect to change the world in just a few months."

"Yes, you can," Hannah shot back, fists balled by her sides. "You start small. That's what you told me. Give back. Make friends. And you don't abandon your friends when they need you!"

Rebekah was looking around her store nervously, but whatever customers had been in there had tactfully left. Aaron's face was flushed, his lips compressed. He no longer looked concerned, but very angry. Hannah's own rage subsided as quickly as it had come upon her. She could tell from the set lines of their jaws that they were fully entrenched in their positions. Nothing she said now would change their minds.

"Please," she said, tears clogging her voice. "Please let me go back once more. I have to say goodbye. They'll wonder where I went.

Please." She uncurled her hands from their tight fists. She stopped trying to stifle the sobs bubbling up her throat, letting them wash over her, her face crumpling, and tears streaming down her cheeks.

"I'm sorry, *gatinha*, I forbid it," Rebekah said, her own eyes glistening. "It's just too dangerous."

CHAPTER 15

Hannah had a hard time readjusting to her life outside of Harry's school. She missed Harry, she missed the boys, but most of all, she missed Bintu. She knew if she bumped into any of them out and about—at the market, on the street, in her mother's store—she couldn't say hello. It would be improper but, more than that, it might endanger them if she did.

Her mother noticed her morose lethargy and kept a hawk's gaze on her, alternating her expressions between worry and exasperation. Rebekah had never been one to abide self-pity. The problem was that Hannah wasn't feeling pity, especially not for herself. Instead, she was fuming with righteous indignation. The girl's wrath was bubbling just below her surface, like lava under a thin scrim of rock.

Hannah was scared that she would lash out at her mother, Levi, Uncle Aaron, or the goblins, or maybe some customers at the store. She wasn't mad at any of them in particular; she was just *mad*, mad at the world and the way it was.

Well, that wasn't entirely true. She was annoyed that her family seemed to accept the injustices of the world while at the same time preaching honor and decency and, above all, justice. *Justice*, the word stuck in her throat like a chicken bone.

But that was how things worked in Charles Town. And since Charles Town was all the world that Hannah knew, it was the way her whole world worked.

Instead of going to the school and helping Harry and Bintu, she was set to her usual tasks at home and in the store. She was tutored in the mornings in the small room her mother used as an office, learning Hebrew, working on her mathematics and a smattering of other subjects she could barely be bothered to pay attention to. The only one who seemed to understand how she felt was King Sol, who had not left her side since she'd come home from Harry's, but was always there, never demanding, but softly leaning against her leg or putting a paw on her foot to show his sympathy. Sometimes she caught him staring out the window and wondered if he too missed their friend.

Hannah was mostly effective in her tasks at the store, mainly because they took much less brain power than teaching, allowing her to let her thoughts wander. She half-heartedly scooped flour or measured precious sugar into smaller sacks for their customers, all the while wondering what was happening at Harry's. If her mother criticized the haphazard way she swept the hearth or bundled cotton cloth, Hannah merely shrugged and waited for her next task. If her mother wanted her to feel deeply about her life and its everyday occurrences, then maybe Rebekah should take a long hard look at her own priorities, Hannah thought, although she would never say something quite so damning to her mother, not in those words.

Hannah felt the sting of her simmering anger daily. She felt as if she was living her life among hypocrites, and hypocrites, she decided in all her thirteen-year-old wisdom, were the worst of all of them. At least Mistress Harte had the decency to not hide her hideousness. She was who she was, in all her hateful glory. Hannah could at least understand her line of reasoning. In her own miserable manner, Mistress Harte was true to herself in a way that Hannah's mother and uncle were not.

She wished her father was back from his interminable journey; she longed for another adult to talk to, to see if they had a measure of decency that she felt the others lacked. She could barely stand it, and felt like jumping out of her skin most days, but especially during services, when the elders spoke about the religious freedom Jews had found in the colonies. She bristled anytime they spoke of any sort of freedom. In her mind, in a community in which slavery was accepted and practiced, no one was free. *What are they playing at? Who do they think they're fooling?*

They weren't fooling Hannah, not anymore. In her mind, if Bintu and the boys weren't free, nobody was.

Hannah's anger came to a head on a rainy afternoon in mid-August. It wasn't just rainy, it was borderline hurricane weather, which, being tidewater flats in late summer, wasn't out of the ordinary. The branches whipped around in swirling gusts and bright green leaves flew through the weird twilit afternoon light, plastering themselves onto the rippled glass pane of the store's front window.

Rebekah had Hannah sorting eggs, which arrived in an oversized basket from a neighbor whose chickens were particularly noisy but also productive. The eggs then had to be sorted into smaller parcels to be sold to separate households. Hannah was trying to be gentle about it, knowing she would get a harsh scolding if she broke an egg with her carelessness. It was difficult though, as she was irritable almost all the time. The act of hiding it constantly set her teeth on edge and made her liable to clumsy, hurried gestures.

Hannah didn't even know her mother was beside her, watching her movements, until Rebekah reached out a hand to place on top of Hannah's, stilling her. Hannah looked up into Rebekah's piercing gaze and then Hannah lowered her eyes after a few seconds. She felt as if her mother could read all the simmering rage and resentment in one glance.

"Hannah," her mother started, "what's the matter? You seem so tense." Her mother spoke carefully, as if she could crack the girl like an egg.

"I'm not, Mother. I'm fine," Hannah replied. She tried to continue her task, but her mother's hand stayed on top of hers, preventing her from further movement.

"Hannah, you can't hide your distress from me. I'm your mother. I can tell, just like when you fib."

Hannah said nothing.

"Is it Harry's School?" her mother asked. "Is that what this is about?"

"Yes," Hannah said, with more emotion than she had estimated. She suddenly felt herself on the brink of tears. "I . . . I miss them, Mama." She surprised herself even more by throwing herself into her mother's arms, almost tipping the woman over with the force of her embrace.

"There, there," Rebekah murmured, stroking Hannah's curls back from her temple. "It was always an impermanent arrangement. You knew that when you started."

They stayed there for a few minutes, Hannah sobbing into Rebekah's shoulder, her mother stroking her hair, and the violent wind lashing the outside of the store fiercely enough to lift the shingles. Hannah was crying so hard that she gave herself the hiccups, sucking in gulps of air between her loud, violent bursts.

Rebekah handed her a handkerchief and Hannah blew her nose until it made a honking sound. Luckily, they were the only ones at the store at the moment; the weather had kept all their customers at home.

Rebekah nodded and grabbed a spoon out a drawer. She went over to a shelf and brought down a stoneware jar of honey, her go-to cure for hiccups.

"Well," Rebekah said, unstopping the lid and dipping the teaspoon in, "what did you think? That you would stay there forever?"

She held up the spoon dripping with golden, viscous liquid and Hannah dutifully opened her mouth. She knew the drill, having been subjected to this cure many times in her childhood. The honey was achingly sweet on her tongue and throat and made her tonsils itch.

"No," she said around the teaspoon in her mouth. She took it out and handed it back. "I didn't think that. I know I don't belong there. I belong here. I know that." She felt the tears start up her throat again and pushed them back down. "But, Mama, I'm worried! Really worried! About Harry, and the boys, but mostly about Bintu."

Her mother put the lid back on the honey, satisfied that her cure had worked. "Why's that?"

"It's that horrible Mistress Harte!" Hannah wailed, feeling not thirteen but three. The tears were back, and Hannah didn't know if she had the strength to stop them. "I wish I could go back one last time to check on her, on them."

Rebekah was very still, and Hannah watched as her mother's face changed like the dusk coming down on a forest, little by little, and then all at once. "Maybe you can."

Hannah's breath stopped in her chest, clogged up by honey. It wasn't the hiccups again, but surprise and hope.

"Do you mean it, Mother?" Hannah asked her, not quite daring to believe the words. "It would mean the world to me, just to see them, one more time."

Her mother was slow to answer as she considered the pewter teaspoon, turning it over and over in her hands. "Would it really mean so much to you?" Rebekah asked, looking up at her daughter through the curls escaping her bonnet. Hannah was struck by how young her mother appeared in that moment, as if they'd somehow swapped places. She nodded fiercely, her own curls bobbing.

Rebekah sighed. "All right. One more time, Hannah, to say goodbye. But that's it. Promise."

"I promise." Her heart leapt as she reached out to take her mother's hand with her own cold one. "Thank you. Why did you change your mind?"

"Because I know her, I know that girl, and I think she's lovely. And I don't stand for Mistress Harte's behavior. Mistress Harte lets emotions rule her reasoning, which is unlucky for anyone standing in her path. I've changed my mind about you going to the school, only the one time, mind you, because it's the right thing to do."

"It's only one more time," Hannah said. "What could happen?"

CHAPTER 16

They came for him during the mid-day meal, an hour after Hannah had arrived to say her last goodbyes. Afterwards, all Hannah could think was, *Those poor boys.* Mealtime was their favorite, mainly because the stew at school was sometimes the only food they would get all day. And now it would be forever ruined. Lunchtime would remind them of this moment when the men showed up.

All the children had been gathered around the battered table or perched on overturned buckets, spoons poised over their steaming bowls, eyes wide in anticipation. Hannah had just handed Washington, a boy of twelve, his bowl of stew when a hammering started up on the door.

"Harry!" hollered a gruff voice. "Open up!"

In a minute, a bewildered Harry appeared at the bottom of the rickety stairs that led up to his living quarters, a book held against his chest. The hammering came again, so hard paint chips showered the ground at the base of the door.

Harry looked at his class, meeting Hannah's eyes last. He mouthed, "Take care," cutting his eyes toward the gathered students before placing his book down on the step behind him and walking to the door with rigid dignity.

He stood before the door and straightened his waistcoat before swinging it open. Two men immediately muscled their way through the frame. They dwarfed everyone else in the room. One had a bunch of dark red curls gathered at the base of his neck like a fistful of red flowers, and the dark-haired one limped. They glanced at the terrified students before stepping up to Harry, each of them grabbing an elbow.

"Hey!" Harry said, twisting out of their grasp with a yank. "Hey, what are you doing? This is a school, and I am the headmaster! You can't maul me." He straightened to his full height, eyes blazing. "This is my school."

When the redhead went to grab him again, Harry danced backwards out of his reach.

"Now, listen here, we're taking you to the hospital," growled the redheaded man, revealing blackened teeth, "You've been acting mighty strange. There are folks who want to see you get better. You a little too cocky for some in town. Time in the hospital should fix you right up."

Harry's eyes darted around the room, weighing his options. Hannah thought he might make a break for the back garden, but that would leave these two men—the dark-haired one was leaning up against the door jamb cleaning his nails with a pocket knife—alone with two girls and fourteen school boys. She knew he wouldn't do that. Who knew what these men would do to them in Harry's absence?

"Who sent you? Why are you here?" Harry protested.

The redheaded ruffian scoffed. "We can make this painful or not. Which will it be?"

Harry ignored him. "Regardless of who sent you, there is nothing wrong with me, and I am not going anywhere until I have finished my duties here. I have no idea what this is about, but I won't stand for it."

The dark-haired one took a languid step toward Harry, knife

in hand, and as Harry stepped back in alarm, the redhead swung a meaty fist into Harry's stomach.

Harry doubled over with a *whuff*, gasping. Hannah dropped the ladle she was using and started toward him, but Bintu grabbed her shoulder.

"No!" Bintu whispered. "Don't!"

Harry, doubled over, held up a hand before painfully straightening. "Tell your superiors," he rasped, "that I will visit them at my leisure, and not a moment before."

"I guess it will be painful then. A little time with the bluejay is what he needs," the redhead muttered to his dark-haired cohort. "You've had it too soft, school teacher, too soft by far."

At the word *bluejay*, Harry's coffee-colored complexion paled. He whipped his head around at the girls. In his absolute terror, Harry looked nothing like himself.

They'd all heard stories about the hospital. It began as a workhouse to care for poor people, but those were gentler times. Now the place had become a repository for runaway slaves and misfits considered too unruly to be dealt with in any other way. Life was terrible there; it was described as a dungeon with cells only as big as closets where a person never saw the light of day. Slaves were punished with the bluejay—a demonic device made of leather with two lashes. At the end of each, a heavy ball laced through with bits of metal hung heavily, ready to inflict pain and misery. It was said that the bluejay not only tore the flesh, but left divots.

Both men stepped toward Harry, who had his hands up in surrender. The redhead grinned as he advanced toward the terrified schoolteacher.

"C'mon there, Harry," the dark-haired one cajoled in a sing-song voice. "No need to make a spectacle."

"Wait a minute," Harry sputtered. "Who would want to send me to the hospital? I've had nothing but success with this school. My patrons agree! There's never been anything that would cause them displeasure."

The two toughs were only a few feet from Harry now, and still advancing. He stepped backwards to put distance between them, and his back hit the lectern he taught from. As the two men came within striking distance, Harry swung quickly around, putting the lectern between himself and the glaring, glowering pair.

"Well, you've caused someone displeasure, that's clear," the dark-haired one said. "The orders were handed straight down from the top, boy. There's no mistake."

"Well, you've got to check again!" Harry's voice cracked in desperation. "There must've been a mistake. I'm telling you, go check again!"

The last remark sounded so much like an order that the dark-haired man paused and cocked his head, a dull red suffusing his face, hinting at rage.

"No, Harry," he said in a brutally quiet voice, closing the distance between them with two long steps. "It's you who's mistaken. You're to be taken to the hospital, and I'm the one who'll be taking you there."

Hannah glanced down. Sukey—a wisp of a boy, just eight years old—was stuck to her skirt like a baby possum, his head buried in the calico cloth. She patted the back of Sukey's head and, when he looked up at her, Hannah saw in his eyes the same terror she'd seen in Harry's. Tears streamed down his cheeks like rain on a windowpane, but he didn't make a sound. Bintu wiped the tears coursing around his nose, and he buried his face back in her skirts, too scared to watch his hero be taken away, but not before she'd seen something else in his face—dull, painful recognition.

This isn't the first time he's had to watch someone he loves being horribly mistreated, Hannah thought. She looked around the room at the knots of silent boys still holding their soup bowls, to Sukey's curved spine poking through his thin shirt, shaking with sobs, to the rigid fury outlining the sharp angles of Bintu's face. Hot bile splattered up her throat, burning her tongue.

The two thugs and Harry were still in a stand-off, Harry keeping his lectern between them. The brutes, whose only language was violence, looked almost bored. At least the dark-haired one did. But Hannah could tell that the boredom was an artifice, and he was very, very angry at Harry's impudence. They'd all been too long in the safe bubble of the school, she and Bintu and the boys and even Harry. They'd forgotten how their world actually worked. The redhead grinned in a hellish contortion of his cracked lips, mightily enjoying himself. Hannah didn't know which was worse, one man's look of boredom or the other's look of mirth.

All at once, the redhead went for Harry, closing the distance between them with one lunge. Harry yelped, Sukey cringed even further into her skirt, and then the thug had Harry. The sudden movement stirred the air in the schoolroom, and Hannah could smell the strange men's scents—tobacco, whiskey, and something swampy.

The redhead clamped his meaty fist around the upper half of Harry's left arm and yanked, like he was marshaling an unruly farm animal. The muscles of his forearm bulged against his shirt cuff—a small hard ball of muscle—and Harry was pulled off his feet like a rag doll and tripped, spilling into his attacker. The red-haired man spun Harry quickly around so that he was suddenly faced with the dark-haired one again.

"Well, hello," the darker man said. "Remember me?" In his left hand he flourished a coil of hairy rope, which he tried to flip a loop of over Harry's wrists.

Harry's wide eyes flicked to the scores of petrified boys. Marcus, the one closest to the fracas, had forgotten his bowl in his hands and the rim dipped, stew spilling over the edge. Hannah's heart ached at that stewy puddle. Marcus rarely had enough to eat for a boy growing as quickly as he was, and he was always ravenous. She had never seen him turn down food or return anything but an empty plate.

Focusing on his boys had instilled some new vigor in Harry. He snapped his mouth shut and clenched his jaw. With an upward surge of strength, he broke the redhead's hold on his arms and stamped, viciously hard, on the man's foot just behind his own. Now it was the redhead's turn to yelp and, as he stumbled backwards, he swiped the lectern, sending it to the ground with a clatter.

The dark-haired man's eyebrows came down in one savage motion and he stepped to Harry, positioned his feet just so, and brought his fist up into the point of Harry's chin in an unstoppable uppercut. Harry's eyes flew up, showing the whites, as he went down hard, like a sack of flour. He hit the wooden floor with a thump, his head bouncing once off the floorboards, and lay still. Someone screamed. Marcus dropped his bowl of stew onto the floor and grabbed Edgefield, covering his mouth with a broad hand. Edgefield cut off his scream, but a dark spot had appeared on his pants and a puddle of urine grew at his feet. The poor child had wet himself in terror.

The redhead recovered, looking abashed, and slapped the other thug on the back. "Nice work, Peter."

"Well, I couldn't let him treat us like that, now, could I?" Peter returned, crouching and wrapping the coarse rope around the unconscious man's wrists.

Once he'd trussed Harry up, he hoisted the rope over his shoulder and pulled Harry toward the door and the waiting wagon outside. Harry's lovely waistcoat, the only one he had and painstakingly cared for, collected chalk and sawdust as he was dragged across the floor. Peter didn't even stop when he reached the door jamb. He simply stepped over it and yanked Harry's body after him. The redheaded man followed and, at the last, turned and looked at Hannah. Fear flared inside her at the hard, blunt force of his gaze.

"As for you, girl, you get you home," he snarled, jabbing a stubby pointer finger at her, "and don't come back. This place ain't suited to the likes of you."

Hannah had no response. She was so furious with the man while at the same time so scared of him that all language vanished like droplets of water in a hot skillet.

"Next time we come here to check up on things, I don't want to find you. D'ya understand?" he asked as his grey eyes blazed across the expanse of the room.

Why was he so angry with her? Was it because he recognized her as Jewish? What had she done? It was he who'd come here, disrupting their lunch, and spilling violence among them. Hannah felt tears spring like hot thorns, but she would not let them fall. She'd be damned if the man saw he'd made her cry. She managed to nod at him, once.

The redhead, satisfied, left the schoolhouse to join the other at their wagon. Through the windows they watched as they grabbed Harry's legs and bound hands, swung him back, and then up in an arc. Harry's inert form cleared the centerboard and he landed in the back of the wagon with a harsh thump and a moan. The two men jumped up to the wagon's seat, grabbing the reins and yelling, "Ha!" to the horse, who jerked out of its reverie and flung itself into a trot.

The students, frozen, watched the wagon carve a large circle in the school's front yard and head off toward town. The dark-haired one even gave them a jaunty wave as they pulled by the open doorway. As soon as they were out of sight, the boys broke and swarmed Bintu and Hannah in a frenzy, all speaking at once.

"Where'd they take Mister Harry, Miss Hannah?"

"Miss Bintu, are they coming back? They said they were coming back?"

"Mister Harry, did they hurt him? It looked like they hurt him!"

These questions peppered the girls like hailstones. The boys' faces and hands were all around them, reaching out, plucking at their skirts, pleading with them. Marcus had moved away from the group, his eyes sparkling with tears, and stood sullenly looking out the window after the wagon that had taken Harry away.

Hannah looked at Bintu over the boys' heads and met her gaze. Neither of them responded to the boys' inquiries. They couldn't. There was absolutely nothing they could say.

As Bintu gathered the boys closest to her in an awkward group hug, Hannah stared out the door into the courtyard, watching the cloud of dust kicked up by the departing wagon dissipate on the late summer breeze, leaving empty space.

When the wagon dust had finally settled, all that could be heard was the sniffle and uneven breath of the boys and the lovely birdsong outside. After a few minutes of collective grief, Bintu stood up and shook her head, picking up the disregarded ladle at her feet, gesturing to Marcus with it before stirring the cooling stew.

"Here now," she said as the boy shuffled over. He stood almost a head taller than both Bintu and Hannah and was thin as a reed. He was swaying like one too, a detached look on his face as he handed over the wooden bowl.

A wail started up behind Hannah. She turned to find Sukey, with his back against the bench, head between his knees.

Hannah crouched down. "Now Suke," she said in a low voice. The boy stopped his caterwaul but didn't lift his head. Hannah waved her hand at Bintu, who put a new bowl of stew in her grasp a moment later. Hannah brought the bowl close to Sukey's head, hoping the smell might shift his focus. She was right; he soon lifted his head, eyes bright and bloodshot, and took the bowl. She found a spoon on the table and handed it to him. A moment later, he began to eat.

The other boys started moving around, picking up discarded spoons and bowls. Washington made sure to pick the lectern up off the ground and set it in its accustomed place, in front of the indentation depressed into the schoolhouse floor where Harry had walked the wood away, pacing in front of his classes.

Crawford, a short broad boy around eleven who was one of their longest-attending students, walked with his head down to the stairs leading up to Harry's quarters. Hannah was about to say something about leaving Harry's rooms be when she saw Crawford reach down for the abandoned book Harry had been reading only ten minutes before. He picked it up, walked over to the lectern, and left it open to Harry's page.

"Miss Hannah?" Sukey had finished his soup and was looking up at her. His eyes were so very old, but his lower lip trembled like a child.

"Yes, Sukey?" Hannah said, easing the bowl from him.

"What will happen to the school? Will it cl . . . close?" A tremor shook his last word.

Hannah's heart ached. She looked over at Bintu. "I don't know, Sukey. I don't know what's going to happen." She gave him another pat on the head.

"We can't let it close, Hannah," Bintu said, one hand still gripping the ladle, which dripped onto the floor. "These boys, they won't have anything else to look forward to if this school closes. This is a place where they can feel safe, if only for a moment. And without that . . . " Bintu trailed off and shrugged. "I know how they feel. It's not just for them but for me too. This school and everyone in it are the only nice things in my horrible new life."

Hannah was astonished, her tongue a strange creature in her mouth. She looked around at all the eyes boring into her, awaiting her response, each with a small spark of hope. Even Marcus, still standing sentinel at the window, was watching her from the corner of his eye. She opened her mouth to tell them that it wasn't a good idea, that it was dangerous, but nothing could make her say those words. Snuffing out even a small flicker of hope would break something in them irrevocably, she felt, and it would break something in her as well. Something that couldn't be fixed.

"No," she said finally, and the fine-tuned hum in the room loosened its grip a little. "No, we won't let it close. Bintu and I will keep it open. Just 'til Harry gets back." She met Bintu's gaze across the room as the boys began to clean, even picking up their playful chatter as they worked.

The girls nodded at each other across the boys' heads. They would keep that school open, the two of them, until Harry came back. Or until someone else came to shut it down.

CHAPTER 17

Rebekah was curious and eager to hear all about Hannah's day when she returned from Harry's that afternoon. This was tricky, uncharted territory for Hannah. She knew that her mother wouldn't let her keep the school open without Harry. That was impossible. It was dangerous for two young girls, one of them a slave, to run a school unsupervised. Rebekah had already made it clear that she was against Hannah spending any more time at Harry's school, and if she learned that some thugs had come in and dragged Harry away, there would be no possibility of Hannah's return.

So Hannah lied, counting on her mother's almost compulsive need to help those in need. It was the first time in her memory that she had told a serious lie to her mother. She had tried bending the truth slightly in the past, but it only took Rebekah one or two follow-up questions to put a stop to the whole business. Her mother claimed that her superb maternal sensitivity always told her when Hannah was hiding the truth. It was either that or that Hannah usually turned bright red, cheeks like polished apples, whenever she tried to fib.

This time it was different. This wasn't a lie about who had churned the butter too long or who'd cut King Sol's whiskers; this time it was deadly serious. The desperation in those boys' eyes kept her face from giving her away.

"Harry's so sick, Mama," she said smoothly. "Please let me help Bintu run the school, just until Harry gets back on his feet." It wasn't a complete lie, she reasoned with a squirming stomach. They *were* waiting for Harry. "He'll be there, just recuperating upstairs. He can help us from there with the students' lessons."

"Oh goodness!" Rebekah exclaimed. "What's he got? Not dyspepsia, I hope. Can I send anything?"

"He says it's his throat," Hannah said, picking out the idea like plucking a leaf from a tree. "He can't speak, he's all hoarse!"

"Some slippery elm then, and ingredients for a hot toddy. Can you tell him to gargle salt water? Tell him from me?"

Relief coursed through Hannah's limbs. Her mother was at the very least going to let her go back long enough to relay this message. Hannah was lucky in that her mother had a very soft heart and could rarely refuse a person in need. She nodded and, when her mother turned away to begin building a basket for Harry, shame finally reddened Hannah's cheeks. She looked down, face burning, enveloped in strange new sadness.

So, under the guise of helping Harry out, Hannah and Bintu were able to keep the school open. Every day, Rebekah sent a new assortment of goodies for poor, sick Harry, and Hannah dutifully carted them to the yellow schoolhouse, her basket made heavier each time by the added guilt she felt by keeping up this farce.

They weren't teaching the boys much; they were really biding their time until Harry got back or until something else happened. After a few days, the boys had healed enough to understand that, without their headmaster, the school would be shut down eventually, either when they stopped showing up or because the authorities would send toughs to shut them down.

Although Hannah wasn't much of a praying type, and she and Bintu had been raised inside entirely different religions, they both actively and audibly prayed that the situation would not end in the latter. The idea of those ruffians coming back was most terrifying.

Bintu and Hannah kept up appearances for the boys. They greeted them in the morning, and set them to work on something, anything, to take their minds off Harry's absence. It was late summer in the tidewater flats of Charles Town. The cicadas had hatched, and their whirring cry filled the somnolent days. Sometimes it felt too hot to even sweat. And, of course, a school day meant a day out of the fields.

Bintu and Hannah had watched Harry enough to set the boys to task, reciting passages and recognizing words and letters on the slates. They would feed them a communal lunch made from food from the garden out back or the boys' tiny plots. Lunch was a much more sober affair since Harry had been taken the week before, but still much loved. The boys left mid-afternoon to put in hours of work to make up for those lost in the schoolroom. None complained, though, as it was easier to work in the late afternoon than in the middle of a hot, swampy August day.

The thugs did show up again, exactly a week and a half after Harry had been taken. It was, once again, their lunch hour, and Bintu was, again, serving up stew. When the hard knock came at the door, the scenario was so similar to Harry's abduction that Hannah briefly felt as if the intervening time had been a dream. One look at the dusty lectern with its untouched book reminded her that, of course, this was not the case.

Bintu and Hannah exchanged terrified glances as Hannah started for the door. She took a steadying breath with her hand on the latch and opened it two inches, putting her eye up to the crack, booted foot set securely behind the door.

Outside in the scorching sunlight were two bulky shapes. As Hannah opened the door an inch wider, the dark-haired one stepped up, put his shoulder to the wood, and pushed. Hard.

Despite her foot, Hannah fell backwards into the room. A few of the boys squealed in fear. She hit the floor with a thud and all the air *whooshed* out of her lungs. The door slammed open to reveal two men, the bright light behind them obscuring their identities. Even though their faces were hidden in shadow, there was no question as to who they were, or what they were doing here. They'd promised to return for the girls, for Hannah specifically, and here they were. And here she was, helpless at their feet.

Hannah's heart clenched as she scanned the darkened planes of their faces for the redhead's ruddy complexion and mirthless grin, he who had so pointedly threatened her the last time. But thankfully, he wasn't there. The dark-haired one was—Peter, she remembered— and it was he who loomed over her as she lay sprawled on the floor. The other one took a few steps into the room, looking around with glittering eyes.

"Who's in charge?" he asked.

With a madly beating heart, Hannah raised her hand. The rest of her students and Bintu were all enslaved, so she would probably get the least severe beating of all of them.

The man, who was medium height, darkly tanned, and largely forgettable, guffawed. "What, you? But you're just a girl." He twisted the last word in an ugly way.

She got to her feet, swaying a little, but looked right at him, dusting her apron off. "I'm in charge," she said with no inflection.

The man laughed harder, putting his hands on his knees and leaning over, eyes closed. Hannah stood stoic as a statue and waited. She was ready for it—the grab, the punch in the gut, the push to the floor, the sack over her head. Whatever was coming at her, better she got it than the boys.

She knew Bintu would also take a beating for these boys, but Bintu had a new bruise every day. Hannah couldn't bear watching her get beaten, not if she could stop it or take her place. She might not be able to save Bintu from horrible Mistress Harte, but she could spare her whatever misery these men had brought to their doorstep. Or at least she hoped she could.

Hannah raised her chin a notch and side stepped, putting herself between these thugs and the boys. Defiantly, she crossed her arms over her chest and huffed, "What do you want?"

The man glanced over at his compatriot, Peter, who was leaning on the lectern and once again cleaning his fingernails. Déjà vu swept Hannah for a second time. For someone who groomed himself as much as Peter did, Hannah wondered why he wasn't any cleaner. There were soot or dirt smudges on his jawline, and his dark hair shone with grease.

Hannah realized that she wasn't as scared of them as she had been a minute ago. They were just stupid, unruly, dirt-smudged rogues. Although she was likely smarter, they were more dangerous. On the tail of this revelation, another wisdom came to her, that when fear evaporated, strength usually took its place.

"Well, I'll be. Would you look at that, Sawyer? This one has some sass." Peter smiled with his mouth, but not with his eyes, and took a step toward her, reaching behind his back. "Haven't we met before, you and me?"

Hannah's throat spasmed, killing her mirth, and something dropped behind her, banging onto the wooden floor. This was it; she was going to get killed by this mean man. Her blood would be spilled on these uneven floorboards. She thought of her mother and tried not to cry.

He was close enough that Hannah could smell him—a musty, dry smell with a hint of rot, like moldy rope.

"You look awful familiar, missy. We have met, haven't we? Did we meet here?"

Hannah couldn't breathe or talk, but she nodded.

"I was told to bring this down to the folks in charge here. Is that you? You look too young." He turned to his compatriot, and Hannah felt that conspiratorial wink in her bones. When he pulled his arm out from behind his back, Hannah cringed. But it wasn't the glint of a sharp knife pointed at her belly, but the white blank face of a piece of paper. Her muscles sagged in relief.

"You can write?" he asked, breath hot and sour in her face. "Make your letters?"

She nodded, muted by fear, and took the paper from his outstretched hand, turning to the lectern for writing instruments. Sawyer went outside, briefly blocking the strong noon light as he went over the lintel and dissipated the tension in the room like steam from a kettle.

Hannah retrieved a quill and dipped it into the inkpot on the lectern, silently praying that the ink hadn't dried since Harry last used it. If the ink was dry, they'd all have to scurry around, finding more. And Hannah wanted to get these two gone as quickly as she could. They hadn't touched the lectern since Edgefield had righted it. They'd let it stand sentry, waiting for Harry. But if this paper was what she suspected it might be, then the lectern would stand sentry forever more. Hannah felt certain that she was being asked to sign Harry's death certificate to release his body.

There was ink, thankfully, and as soon as she got the quill tip wet, she shifted her attention to the paper at hand. It took her a moment to realize that the paper was not a death certificate, but a release form. It took a few more moments to figure out that it was from the Charles Town Workhouse. She felt a tremor go through her as her eyes anxiously scanned the document to see if they were releasing Harry's corpse, or Harry himself.

She looked at Bintu at the edge of the half circle of silent boys, hands twisting her apron into tight coils. Then a shadow blocked the light from the doorway again and Sawyer dragged in a large burlap sack and upended it onto the floor. A jumble of arms and legs tumbled out as the body hit the floor facedown. He was wearing the sackcloth of the Workhouse and was almost unrecognizable for all the dried blood, yellowing bruises, and split skin.

It was Harry. Bintu rushed to his side and put her head to his chest. When she raised her face to Hannah's, her eyes shining, she smiled. He didn't look alive, but he was. Barely.

Hannah lay the release form on top of the open book on the lectern and wrote her name at the end of the document with a shaky hand. When she dropped the quill on the book, it rolled off the slope and plunged to the floor, forgotten. She handed the paper to Peter and hurried to Harry, crouching close to his face.

"Harry?" she whispered, and a surge of joy pulsed through her when his eyelids twitched open.

He didn't recognize her, probably couldn't see her through his puffed-up eyes. Every patch of visible skin was mottled by either the purple of fresh bruises or the yellow of old ones. She quickly looped Harry's inert arm around her shoulder, with Bintu at the other side, dragging him to his feet.

"Marcus, Crawford, come help us please," Bintu said. The two older boys rushed over and took the burden of Harry's inert body from them.

They dragged Harry toward his stairs, Hannah and Bintu following close behind. When they reached the bottom, Hannah turned back to the pair of men milling around the doorway. Anger seeped through the last carapace of fear, melting it away.

"Sirs, I believe you have done enough. Please leave." Her voice had absolutely no inflection and she kept her eyes pinned on them. She felt her mother's strength course through her. There was no way she was going to leave them down here with her boys.

The brutes seemed as if they might protest, a dark red creeping out of Peter's collar to stain his neck and cheeks, but finally he harrumphed and walked out the door. Sawyer followed, slamming it behind them.

Harry groaned at the loud noise. He was so broken, like a smashed rocking chair. Marcus and Crawford were able to drag him up the stairs without too much trouble and lay him across his bed on the ancient quilt, the rope beneath the mattress and straw in it squeaking with his weight. He groaned, thrashing weakly and trying to turn over. The boys didn't seem to know what to do, but stood over their fallen teacher, looking forlorn and diminished. Bintu pushed through them to help Harry roll onto his stomach. There were bright blots of new blood on the back of his shirt like poppies, staining the darker patches of old blood.

The bluejay. Hannah gagged at the thought, swallowing down acidic bile. *At least he's alive, and he's back. That's the important thing.*

Bintu laid another threadbare blanket across Harry's inert body and started for the stairs, pushing Crawford and Marcus out of the room as she did so. "A salve," she said, looking at Hannah with haunted eyes. "I have a salve that may help." Then she was gone.

Hannah stood, looking down at the splintered scrap of her teacher, arms wound around her midsection for strength. It seemed impossible that Bintu could have anything in her arsenal of tonics, unguents, and salves to help Harry, who was so shattered. She could barely see his breathing; he looked more like a corpse than a living being.

But it was there, the slight rise and fall of his chest under the loosely woven blanket, proving he was alive.

CHAPTER 18

The next day, Harry was on his feet, albeit unsteadily. Hannah arrived around ten lugging her customary basket. She was glad for the subterfuge she had chosen, that of Harry's sickness. Today, her mother had supplied her with some tinctures for headaches and laudanum for pain as well as a medley of foodstuffs. When she walked in and saw Harry standing at the lectern, book open in his hand, she almost dropped her basket out of surprise, relief, and pure joy.

But he looked so different, moving stiffly as he slowly paced his customary circuit across the rough floorboards. He looked strained around the edges, like he might faint, grimacing in pain. Still, for the boys, he smiled.

From his posture, she guessed it was his back, but it may have been something worse, like broken ribs.

Hannah bustled over to the small table in the back of the classroom and Harry met her there, moving with the careful dignity bred by immense pain. She unpacked her mother's gifts, handing over two fresh lemons instead of storing them. Harry loved lemon water.

As she stowed the items on the long shelves that stretched across the back wall—honey, dried parsley, a jar of rolled oats—she avoided Harry's eyes. She could feel him looking at her, but she kept her gaze pinned to the task at hand. It was only when she finally looked up that she noticed how sad he was. She could tell even through the kaleidoscope of mottled bruises.

"Miss Hannah," he began.

Her heart sank further, hearing his labored voice. "Yes?" she said, overly brightly, fluttering around the table like an anxious hen over a brood of eggs.

"Miss Hannah."

Something in his tone made her stop the façade and look at him and, when she did, the tiny shred of sunny hope that was left to her fled. Whatever it was that he was about to tell her, she guessed would be unwelcome.

"Yes, Harry?" she asked in a small voice.

"It's been so wonderful, having you here. We've all grown very fond of you, Miss Hannah, especially Bintu."

The murmuring of the boys at their lessons subsided and, when she chanced a glance their way, she saw the pairs and trios of boys silent and still, looking at her out of the sides of their eyes or stoically staring at one another while they listened.

"But?" she said. "There sounds like there's going to be a *but.*"

"No buts, Miss Hannah. It has been such a gift, having you here. You've shown these boys something special. That not everyone is cruel and cold-hearted in this world. It's the most important thing you've taught them, and I hope they carry that lesson in their hearts through all their hard lives."

Hannah glowed at his words.

"But?" she said, and Harry smiled softly.

"But I'm afraid your presence here has put you in danger. Grave danger." He watched her face with his purpled eyes to gauge her reaction. "There has never been sentiment against us before. I've been teaching here since the vestry purchased me when I was fourteen. It seems, for the first time in this school's history, that there are those who work against us. People who want to see this school demolished, torn down, or burnt, and for me to be permanently locked up in that place." He shuddered. "I never would've thought, with our long success as a school, that one displeased old nanny goat could tumble us."

"Mistress Harte," Hannah said in a whisper.

"Yes," Harry said, his stained-glass eyes bright.

"So it *was* her. Old Nanny Goat Harte."

Harry snorted ruefully. "I'm not sure if it was her or the vestry or town politics, but Charles Town is changing and not for the better. At least not for us. And not for *you*, Miss Hannah. I don't want you caught in the middle."

Horrible Mistress Harte and her cruel ways, Hannah thought. She remembered how the woman's face had looked as she had left after that first visit. Pinched and triumphant. If Mistress Harte was the type of person to burn and cut a child just because she was beautiful, like Bintu, then she was absolutely the type of woman who would bring down a school because of a social slight. No matter the school's success.

"And now their gaze has turned on you," Harry said. "You are among us, seemingly one of us, a young Jewish girl, daughter of a prominent merchant family. There are plantation owners and merchants that are not happy to learn that you're here with us."

Did he know, she wondered, *about Bintu and me running the school?*

"Bintu told me, of course," he said, reading her thoughts. "They were fond of you and Bintu before, the boys were, but since you kept things going for them, even with me gone— giving them the midday meal, putting them to simple tasks—well, now they adore you both, no doubt about it. For giving them a place to come to that was safe, if just for a few hours each day."

Hannah and Harry looked over at the students. Most ducked their heads, abashed. From his spot in the corner, Washington gave Hannah a small nod, a ghost of a smile gracing his face. No matter what happened next, she was proud of herself and Bintu, for making sure the boys could come here, despite Harry's absence.

"But your time at our school has sadly come to an end, Miss Hannah."

Hannah's stomach clenched as tears welled. Here it was, the meat of it. *But it was always going to come to this,* she thought. *Like Mama said, it was never going to be for long.*

"Harry, all of it, I was glad to do it. It wasn't any trouble. I like to help, and I like you all, so much," she trailed off, not trusting her voice to remain steady.

"I know, I know." Harry looked sorry, under his motley of purple-brown and yellow skin. So sorry. "We care for you too. I do, and that's why I have to send you away." He placed his hands, palms down, on the table and studied them. Then he looked up, sentiment turning his eyes incandescent. "I was told that you and Bintu showed a lot of courage when those thugs came back to return me."

Hannah nodded.

"If Bintu had stood up alone to them, she would've been beaten or maybe worse. Instead, you stood up. Do you remember why you did that?"

Hannah thought about it. "Because I could not bear to watch any of the boys get hurt, or beaten, or taken away. Or Bintu. I just couldn't bear it."

"And I could not bear it if any harm befell you. Do you see? I just couldn't bear it," he paused, letting that sink in for her. "It's fine for me to take the brunt of it, but not my students. And not you."

Hannah remembered raising her hand from her place on the floor when the thug had asked her who was running the place. It was an instantaneous decision; at that moment there had been no other choice. Any punishment they doled out on her would be less dear, in her mind, than having to watch any of the others hurt, or worse. They were all people, all of them, no matter if they were free or enslaved. They could all be hurt and bleed. But what was the use of that? What was the use of any of it?

From the groupings of boys, she heard a sniff. Her chin trembled and she stilled it with her will. She didn't want to cry in front of the boys, but she didn't think she'd be able to repress her tears much longer.

"We'll never forget you, Miss Hannah," Harry whispered, smiling with diamond bright tears in his eyes too. "We have something for you. It's out in the garden with Bintu and Crawford. Bintu is not happy with this turn of events, and you know how headstrong she can be. But what choice is there? For us, as slaves, there's never any choice."

Hannah nodded, still not trusting her voice, and trailed after him, out the back doorway and into the kitchen garden. The scrape of wooden chair legs against the floor behind told her that the boys were following.

Outside stood Bintu and Crawford next to a hole that had been newly dug in one corner of the garden next to the few dry stalks of corn, the moisture of the dark overturned earth slowly drying to a brownish gray. Crawford was holding a shovel and his dark skin was flushed and shiny. Digging was hard work in the coastal heat.

Bintu wasn't looking at her as they approached, but stood still as stone, staring at her feet. Hannah stopped in front of her friend.

"Bintu?"

She only got a glimpse of Bintu's red-rimmed eyes before her arms were full of Bintu's skinny frame, shaking with sobs. Soon Hannah was sobbing as well. Harry and the boys just stood there, waiting and sweating. When the girls parted, Bintu kept Hannah's hand entwined in her own. Hannah wiped her nose on her apron.

To Crawford's left was a small tree, its root ball sitting in a woven reed basket.

"It's a peach tree," Harry told her. "We thought that something that gave us such fruit would be a fitting tribute to you."

Sukey came up beside her. "Mister Harry thought, since you are so generous and kind, that you would like it, because it will give us joy too, like you do. We're going to call it Hannah's Tree."

Hannah's heart expanded, catching in her throat, and she smiled through her tears. "It's wonderful. Thank you. Thank all of you."

Quite a few of the boys had wet eyes. Harry nodded at Crawford, who wrangled the sapling into the hole and shoveled a spadeful of dirt into the hole. He then handed the shovel to Harry, who shoveled another spadeful before handing the shovel to Washington, and so on. Each boy stepped up in turn, each chucking an allotment of earth onto the tree, her tree, Hannah's Tree. When it was her turn, she felt the slick sweat of the others' hands on the handle as she tossed down her own spadeful. The shovel came back around to Crawford and he finished the job, patting the loose earth down pat with the back of the shovel head.

All eyes were on Hannah, waiting for her to say something. She didn't know what to say; her words swelled and stuck in her throat. She walked over to the small tree, so diminutive next to the tall corn stalks, and pulled free the scrap of calico from her hair, letting the curls spring loose. She tied the calico around the tree trunk, double knotting the cloth into a bow.

"Sukey," she said hoarsely, "you must water the tree as it grows, or else it will die. Can you do that? Will you water this tree? Keep it alive?"

Sukey nodded gravely.

"I don't—" she started, as tears swamped her words again. She stood for a moment, her hand at her mouth, collecting herself. "Thank you all. It is such a wonderful gesture." More sniffs came from the group of boys surrounding the small tree. "I will never forget you, any of you. You've all become so much to me. You are truly my friends." Her voice broke on the last word, and she hung her head. Arms wrapped around her waist as Bintu embraced her. Soon she felt other arms around her, all of the boys, *her* boys, wrapping their arms around her and one another. They all stood there in a human knot, sweating and crying. Only Harry stood apart, wiping his eyes.

Hannah left the school soon after they'd planted the tree. There didn't seem to be anything else to say, and she couldn't bear their sad eyes on her all afternoon. She doubted that she'd see any of them again, maybe in passing at the market, but even then, she wouldn't be able to greet them the way she'd like to—let alone hug them. This was it, and they all knew it.

As the schoolhouse's creaky door closed behind her, severing her from them with an irrevocable *click*, Hannah felt the weight of separation settle on her shoulders. She walked slowly back to her mother's store, dragging her feet through the dust, as the day deepened into a beautiful summer afternoon, the trees tossing their heads in gusts of wind and dragonflies whizzing by on their way to the river.

As she walked, she thought more about Bintu. There had been two new welts on the side of Bintu's face today, and she cringed when Hannah had hugged her, as if in pain. Beyond the sadness of having to leave Harry's, now that it had finally come to pass, Hannah recognized something new. She was scared—no, terrified—that her friend would be scarred and burnt or worse at the hands of old Nanny Goat Harte.

During her sad retreat through the afternoon, Hannah realized a truth—she had to help Bintu get free, any way she could. This resolution didn't make her feel any better. In fact, she never felt more alone in her life.

CHAPTER 19

Three days later, Hannah and Rebekah were having a stormy discussion that escalated into a squall. They had closed shop and were out in the back, preparing a cold dinner. The light lengthened into golden shafts in the early September evening, dispelling the worst heat of the day into a sumptuous tidewater flat twilight.

The conversation had begun innocently enough. When Hannah fetched up a long sigh while sorting butter beans, her mother, feet up on a stool, had asked her what was the matter.

"The matter is Bintu. I'm just worried about my friend, is all," Hannah grumped, shoving the beans around the inside of the bowl.

Perhaps she was being impertinent, but she had put in a long day in the shop too. King Sol stopped washing his paws and looked up at her, as if even he could recognize her insolent tone.

"Watch yourself, Hannah," Rebekah warned. "Do not deign to use that impudent tone of voice with me. I am not the guilty culprit here." When Hannah's mother got angry, which she rarely did, she began using her largest words, as if her vocabulary was an arsenal and her biggest words, her strongest weapons. Hannah's father often joked that he realized he was in deep trouble when four-syllable words started pouring forth from Rebekah's mouth.

Hannah knew she should tread carefully here, her mother had warned her, but she couldn't help it. She'd been mad for days, ever since Harry had sent her away. The angry lava came bubbling up, and there was nothing Hannah could do to stop it.

"I can't help it, Mama! It's just so unfair! Bintu was stolen, *stolen*, from her home, sent to a new country never to see her family again, given a new name, and punished almost every day for no apparent reason. She is property, like how this table is property." She slammed her palms onto the table, making the butter beans jump. "And yet every Saturday we go to services, and I hear about how this is the land of the just and the free. I hear how everyone in the colonies are equal, and all can make a fresh start. And I know now that it's not true!"

Rebekah was astonished. "Hannah, child, calm yourself." She reached out a hand, but Hannah ripped her arm away.

"No, I won't calm myself. Not when my friend's life is in danger, just because her mistress decided she didn't like her!" Hannah studied her hands for a moment to catch her breath. Should she tell her mother what she knew? She decided now was the time, more than any other moment. She could feel it in the very marrow of her bones.

"Bintu told me about another slave in the house, who got branded by Reverend Harte." Hannah let that sink in. "She said Mistress Harte attended the branding and smiled the whole time. Smiled and showed her teeth, cheerful as a canary. When it was done, Bintu said she'd asked the Reverend, 'Isn't there any more you can do to her?'"

Rebekah looked green around the gills.

"What if Mistress Harte kills Bintu? What then, Mama? Will we all just forget she existed?" Her mother looked away, clenched fist to her lips, and Hannah knew she had to press her final point. "Will she even be buried? Have a gravestone? Will *her* mother even know that her daughter is dead?"

Rebekah's bodice was moving fast with her breathing, and she looked absolutely forlorn. But Hannah didn't care; she may never get the chance to say her piece and speak up for Bintu ever again. Somebody had to speak up for her. Hannah considered Bintu her best friend—perhaps her *only* one. She had to make this moment count.

"She was stolen, Mama, from her home and her family. They stole her and took her far, far away. She has no one to protect her here. She's all alone. That is, she was, until she met me." Hannah's fury left her suddenly, like water through a sluice. She was spent. She uncurled her fists and the blood rushed back into her hands, making them tingle. "But then I abandoned her too."

She slowly sank back down in her seat. "Am I just to pretend that we live a decent and honorable life when I know that there are good people, neighbors—like Bintu and Harry—that suffer everyday while we ignore it? It's not fair. It will never be fair."

Hannah waited for the reprimand, the smack across the cheek, the harsh condemnation. But after a few moments, there was none. She looked up at her mother and was shocked to see tears in Rebekah's eyes. Hannah reached out her hand to her mother, who smiled shakily and took it.

"You're right, Hannah. You're absolutely right."

Hannah was speechless. She hadn't expected her mother to agree with her tirade.

"But, *gatinha*, there's nothing we can do about it. It's just the world we live in."

"Maybe it's a world I don't *want* to live in. You've always told me that one kind act can change the world, Mama. Now you're telling me different? Hypocrite!" she spat out the word, and Rebekah flinched.

Hannah stood and stalked toward the doorway that opened into their backyard. She stopped as she reached it and turned, mustering all the self-control she could.

"Well, Mama, I refuse to accept it. I won't. It's wrong. It's not fair.

And my friend, she's getting hurt or worse all the time. I won't accept that. I have to do something about it."

With that, Hannah left her mother looking after her, her dark eyes wide, and went across the narrow yard and into the house, and then into her refuge atop the house.

Earlier in the year, Rebekah had finally acquiesced and let Hannah move into the attic, a request Hannah had been pummeling her with for years. It was a relief for Hannah to have her own space after living most of her life bunking with Levi. He wasn't a terrible little brother, but he was a terrible snorer, sounding like an asthmatic barn animal on the best of nights.

Even though the attic was too hot in the summer and too cold in the winter, Hannah loved it, despite having to duck her head to avoid bumping it on the eaves whenever she got into or out of bed. She was growing quickly, so quickly she was even outgrowing her own room, it seemed.

After her momentous outburst, Hannah tumbled up the attic stairs and flung herself onto her bed, quite sure that she'd soon hear her mother's steps on the stairs to Hannah's attic.

Despite her fear, Hannah was ready for whatever punishment her mother was going to dole out, strengthened by her own belief that what she'd said was true. But there was nothing, and after half an hour of listening to the leaves tap at the windowpane, inches away from where her head lay on her pillow, Hannah fell asleep.

The next morning, Hannah opened her eyes to grey skies and rain washing down her window. Hannah got up, rinsed off her face with the tepid water from the ewer at her bedside, and headed downstairs to face the music.

Hannah expected a furious backlash peppered with many four-syllable words from her mother. But, to her surprise, Rebekah was oddly quiet, speaking only the bare minimum. She hadn't meant to unleash all her anger on her mother. In her quiet time alone, Hannah acknowledged that Bintu's situation wasn't her mother's fault. But she had no one else to talk to about it, and she'd needed to vent, to get it out of her system like an infection.

She meekly peeked into the store, looking down the long narrow aisle that led to the front counter, but there was no one. She gathered her courage, grabbed her full apron and skirt in both hands, and stepped off the last stair. Hannah entered the store, timid and chastened.

There were a few people in the long room, escaping the rain. Hannah walked down the dry goods aisle, skirts brushing the stacked cotton bolts, until she arrived at the counter at the front. She usually worked on the near end of the scarred wood table, and Rebekah's cash box crouched at the other end like a metal toad. Her mother was behind the counter adding up Mistress Harby's weekly order, with the old woman in front of her, undoubtedly adding up the prices in her head at the same time Rebekah did the figures with chalk on the slate beside her.

"That's twelve cobs and two bits for the flour, three more for the eggs, and eighteen for the sugar," Rebekah said. She hadn't yet looked at Hannah, who stood quietly next to her, waiting and trembling. "I'll put it on your account, Mistress Harby?"

"Eighteen for the sugar!" exclaimed Mistress Harby, placing a gnarled hand on her bodice. "That's a trifle dear, isn't it?"

"There's a new tax on sugar, just like the one we are going to have on paper, Mistress Harby." Rebekah left it at that, and the old woman fussed for a moment before she began counting out coppers onto the counter. It was an old, practiced ritual between them. Rebekah didn't seem to mind the haggling, as long as the Harbys paid in the end.

After Mistress Harby had counted out the requisite sums, Rebekah helped her pack away her stores into a large basket. She finally turned to Hannah, who had to suppress a flinch.

"Hannah, dear," her mother said in her normal voice. Hannah's eyebrows raised an inch. "Would you please take Mistress Harby's wares to her carriage? Moses will be waiting just outside to help you lift it."

Hannah nodded, mystified, and hoisted the heavy basket off the counter. She followed Mistress Harby's bustling skirt to the door and then out into the wild wind. The rain had stopped, but the breeze that pulled at their clothes and tugged their hair from under bonnets was damp and untamed, like a pestering pixie.

"Hannah, hand that over to Moses," Mistress Harby said without turning around. "Mind you, don't drop it before you do. I got eggs." The older woman grunted as she put one booted foot on the step and heaved herself into her carriage in a cascade of slightly yellowed and torn petticoats and lace.

Moses, a large man in a blue, loose shirt and breeches, smiled down at Hannah as he took the basket from her. His hands engulfed the entire handle, making the basket look like it belonged to a doll. Hannah smiled back.

Moses swung the basket into the back of the wagon and the movement briefly recalled the way the thugs at the schoolhouse had swung Harry into the back of their wagon, as if he were merely a sack of flour.

She stood there after they left, the carriage jouncing along the streets that had been recently pockmarked by the falling rain. Moses carefully led their horse around downed branches and the larger potholes, Mistress Harby's shrill voice rattling off instructions to him. The breeze tugged at Hannah's hair. With a sigh, she turned back into her mother's store, the tiny bell above the door heralding her return.

And the bell did not stop dancing over the entry all afternoon. The store was very busy for a Tuesday. The storm, which had doused the area for three days, had kept most people indoors except for the bravest and most desperate. Now necessity had pushed them outdoors, and they had all arrived at Rebekah's store in the lee of the hurricane.

Hannah was set to tasks all afternoon without a moment to talk to her mother in between running here for this customer or fetching that for another. By the time they closed and locked the door, last night's outburst seemed like it had happened days ago.

For supper that evening, the goblins made their weekly appearance at the Cardozo dinner table, and so most of the meal was spent preventing the boys from hurling potato bits at one another, with Levi trying not to laugh as Hannah and Rebekah dodged and parried.

Hannah helped her mother clean up, but whenever she tried to broach the subject, Rebekah shut her down. Much to her relief, she was at least able to apologize for the outburst.

"I'm sorry, Mama, I didn't mean to yell at you like I did."

Rebekah passed her a plate with a dripping hand as her other reached for the next dish in the pile. "I know, but thank you for saying so." Rebekah pulled the kettle over on its long arm and poured steaming water onto the plates in the basin.

"I didn't mean to—" Hannah stuttered. Rebekah stopped her with a hand on her arm.

"Listen to me, Hannah, never apologize for what you believe in. I thank you for apologizing for yelling—nobody likes to be yelled at. But don't apologize for caring for your friend, or speaking out about what's wrong." Rebekah's eyes were bright, which usually meant she was angry, but Hannah could tell from her tone that she wasn't. "Do you understand me?"

Hannah nodded.

"Always stand for what you believe in," Rebekah finished, "or you'll regret it when you're old." She removed her hand, leaving a wet handprint on the arm of Hannah's dress. That was all that was said as they finished the rest of the dishes.

Late that night, up in her attic hideaway, Hannah couldn't sleep. The weather was oddly claustrophobic, like wet cotton batting.

Puffs of wind pried up the edges of the shingles, lifting them up and slapping them down, and in the next moment, dying off completely, leaving the house creaking in the silence.

Hannah pressed her head into the lumpy pillow and finally realized that it wasn't just the wind that was keeping her awake. What had occurred between her mother and herself was still rankling, nibbling at the edges of her consciousness like a hungry mouse. It was as if her mother had seen her as an adult, at least for a moment. And in that moment, Hannah had also been able to really see her mother—imperfect, resolute, tenacious, and loving.

The wind pried at the edges of her attic eaves and then died out. In the silence that followed, she heard them, the bass rumbling of a man's voice floating up the stairs from the living room. She sat up in bed, ready to throw off her covers and bolt down the stairs. *Father! He's returned?*

Common sense trickled through as she realized it couldn't be him. They'd received his last letter just the previous week, and it had been postmarked London, a month before. There was no way he could get back here in that amount of time. She sagged back against the wall in disappointment. It must be Uncle Aaron down there, although why he hadn't joined them for their evening meal she couldn't guess. Rebekah had only invited him after the children had all gone to bed. Because she'd wanted to talk to him alone.

Hannah's hands clenched her sweaty sheets into fists. They must be concocting a just punishment for her; that's why her mother had been so silent on the topic all night. She sat there for a few moments, listening to the murmur of basso in her uncle's voice and a contralto in her mother's until she just couldn't stand it a second longer. She had to hear what they were saying.

She crept out of bed, feet sticking to the humid film on the floor. She padded down the flight of stairs from the attic to the living quarters. Halfway down, she stopped, slowly lowering herself on the least creaky stair, and listened.

"What can I do?" Uncle Aaron said in his rumbly voice. "There are four ways a slave can become free here. The first way is for the girl to buy her freedom, but we know the Hartes will not grant her that. The second way is for the Hartes to grant her manumission and set her free out of the kindness of the hearts."

Rebekah snorted.

"The third way is to buy the girl ourselves, and then set her free. We'll try that first. But if they won't have it, which I don't think they will, there's only one more option left for her."

"Which is?"

"She'll have to run away," Aaron said with finality. "And we will have to help her."

On the stairs, a droplet of sweat trickled down the back of Hannah's neck, making her shiver. She licked her upper lip and tasted salt.

"It's dangerous," her mother said after a lengthy pause. "Especially for the girl. She's the one that will pay the most dearly if caught."

"The girl, Chastity I think the Hartes have named her, will find herself without an ear. Or with her face branded. Or worse."

"Would they kill her, Aaron?"

"No, they won't destroy valuable property. But they'll beat her to within an inch of her life."

Another silence, and in it Hannah heard the wind and her own heart, beating like a frenzied drum.

"But why, Rebekah?" Aaron said softly. "Why risk it at all?"

"Because she's right, Aaron. Hannah is right."

"She's right? What do you mean? She's merely a child."

"She may be young, but she sees clearly enough."

On the stairs, Hannah's heart leapt into her throat. She clutched at the neck of her nightdress.

"We preach about justice, religious freedom, *Tzedek*, all of that," Rebekah admonished, "but we do not practice what we preach. We let injustice happen all around us and do nothing."

"But Rebekah, consider for a moment. This is a very dangerous business. Caught runaway slaves are mutilated, and we would face almost certain ruin."

"I know, Aaron. I have dwelt on this for many days. I feel strongly that if we do not act on this, Bintu will come to harm at the Hartes' hands, and we will have failed Hannah in a way she won't forget or recover from. We risk a lot on either path, but I know which one I think is the right one. In my heart, I know."

Tears came to Hannah. Her mother had listened to her, really listened.

"You should have seen her, Aaron, you would've been so proud. Her eyes blazing, her stubborn chin more set than ever. She really gave it to me."

Aaron's low chuckle echoed up the stairs. "I imagine she looked a lot like you, sister."

"Maybe at one time, but not anymore. I used to be sure of myself, but not if I let this go. And I can't let this go, Aaron. I won't be able to look Hannah in the eye. And truly, it will hurt my heart to see the girl harmed by that witch just for spite. She saved Hannah's life, you know. We owe her. Perhaps we can repay her with her own."

Hannah leaned forward in her eagerness to catch every word. The steps under her feet lightly creaked with the weight. She froze, hoping her mother and uncle would assume it was just the wind.

"The Hartes won't take it lightly, Rebekah," Aaron said after a few moments. "You know what that woman's like. She will make our lives a living hell if she finds out."

"I do know what she's like, which is why we have to help. If we leave that girl there, Agnes will continue to abuse her until she runs away on her own and then she will have an excuse to punish her even more severely. The girl is caught in a vicious web with no way out. All because she's pretty, and her blue eyes caught the Reverend's rheumy old brown ones. Agnes is a vindictive shrew, Aaron, and mean beyond measure."

Hannah's stomach curdled at the idea. Bintu punished so cruelly for her beautiful blue eyes. What poetic injustice.

"Will you do it?" Rebekah's voice was soft, almost tender.

There was a pause so long Hannah thought maybe she missed her uncle's response. When he spoke, his voice was as low as Rebekah's when she was angry. "You think this girl is really in danger, Rebekah?"

Hannah heard nothing, but imagined her mother nodding solemnly.

"And you think if we stand by, and let this happen, we'll lose Hannah as well."

More silence. More imaginary nodding from Rebekah. On the stairs, Hannah bit her knuckle and squinched her eyes shut.

"Fine, I'll do it."

Hannah clapped both her hands over her mouth. He'd agreed!

"Yes. I'll do it. For you, for *Tzedek*, but especially for Hannah."

Rebekah made a sound of joy. "Thank you, brother. For me, and for Hannah."

"I just pray we don't get caught. It might set the whole town aflame."

"Maybe, but if it isn't a missing slave girl, it will be something else. The town is ready to ignite. Any stray spark will do."

"I suppose you're right. How do we tell her, Hannah, I mean? We'll need her help, I assume, to communicate with the Hartes' girl."

"I don't think we'll have to tell her much. She's heard most of it from her spot on the stairs." Her mother's voice rose. "Hannah? Come on down, I know you're there."

Hannah froze for an instant, astonished that her mother found her out so quickly. Then she bashfully descended the last eight steps into the main room. Her uncle was standing by the deadened hearth and her mother was in the rocking chair, facing the stairs' landing. She trotted quickly over to her mother's chair and sat between her and the cold hearth, tucking her nightshirt under her knees.

"Uncle Aaron?" Hannah said, twisting her head to look up at him.

"Yes, Hannah."

"What's *manumission*?"

He chuckled. "So, you were listening closely then, little mouse. Manumission is a slave's freedom. An owner can sign a document that sets a slave free."

"But the Hartes won't do such a thing."

"No, my dear, your mother and I do not think that's possible for the Hartes' girl. Her master and mistress do not have sympathy for many."

"Thought so."

"But there may be something we can do, even if the Hartes do not agree."

They talked until the half-moon had sunk below the sill of the window and the sky had turned a light violet. In their conversation, Aaron and Rebekah asked Hannah serious questions, deferring to her opinion, although Rebekah did keep playing with her daughter's hair, twisting the curls around her finger as she spoke.

At one point, when the church on the corner struck two, one of the goblins, Hannah couldn't tell them apart when they were in their night shirts, stumbled into the main room, whining about being thirsty. Rebekah gave him a drink of water from the pitcher and bustled him down the hall into Levi's bedroom where the other boys still slept. The moment Rebekah disappeared, carrying the small boy into the shadowed hallways, Aaron turned to Hannah with the most serious face she'd ever seen on him. It scared her.

"This is dangerous, Hannah."

"I know."

"It's dangerous for you and me, to be sure. That's why we're asking the Hartes if we can buy her first. That is the easiest. If we bought her, we could simply grant her manumission and then help her leave Charles Town. Or we could help her buy her own freedom. Whichever seemed easiest." Aaron stopped, staring into the swept hearth at his boot toes. "I think Harte won't sell her, or even rent her out. No matter what we say. I don't think it would even cross his mind. It might even strike him as humorous that we suggest it." Another long pause. "Then we are faced with smuggling the girl out or helping her run away. A last resort. It has consequences for everyone involved. But for the girl it is especially dangerous. Maybe even fatal. Do you understand that?"

Hannah nodded. She knew that if they were caught aiding a runaway slave they would be punished severely. But Bintu would be beaten—her ear cut off or her face branded.

"Do you think she knows the risks and the consequences? Your friend?"

Hannah gazed over his shoulder into the semi-darkness. The candles had long ago burnt out. Instead of the half-darkened room around her, she saw the stubborn tilt of Bintu's chin when she'd been up on the auction block the first day Hannah had seen her, the set of her jaw when she had taken the Bateman's Elixir out of Rebekah's hands, the way Bintu's eyes blazed as she watched the thugs drag an unconscious Harry out of school like a sack of onions.

She also thought about the ugly welts and scars Bintu tried so hard to hide from her when they'd been at school together. Those wounds had been inflicted by Agnes Harte and, Hannah remembered with a shudder, had gotten worse and worse as time went on. Who knows what the woman had done to Bintu by now?

"Uncle Aaron," Hannah said, weighing each word. "What you mean is that if they catch her, it will be very bad for her. They will hurt her a lot."

Aaron glanced down the hall toward Levi's darkened bedroom where Rebekah's voice murmured a lullaby. Then he nodded.

Hannah thought for a while, listening to the croon of her mother's voice lulling another woman's child to sleep. "She's going to be hurt either way. Either by old Nanny Goat Harte or because she was caught trying to gain her freedom. Which would you choose? Wouldn't you want a choice?"

"Yes, I see what you mean." Aaron stared at her as if he'd never seen her before in his life. "If the Hartes say no, which I suspect that they will, we must have the girl's agreement. I won't take her unless she fully understands the risks and consequences of her actions."

"That's why she has to give us the sign, the candle in the upstairs window."

It had been decided earlier that Hannah and Aaron would call upon the Hartes to talk about purchasing Bintu. This wasn't their only plan, however.

Neither Aaron nor Rebekah had much hope that Agnes would be willing to part with her favorite toy. Like a cat with wounded prey, it would be hard to get Bintu out of Agnes's claws. So, they'd also concocted a back-up plan if and when the Hartes said no.

Aaron stretched one long leg out and then the other, knees cracking. "You're sure she can read, Hannah? The girl?"

Hannah grinned, and her face transformed from a serious young woman's to a delighted girl's. "Of course, Uncle Aaron! I taught her myself!"

CHAPTER 20

The day they were to visit the Hartes was clearer. The early fall storm hadn't yet wreaked all its havoc on the town, but threatened as its bruised thunderheads loomed low over one part of the harbor.

Hannah and her uncle walked in silence, skirting puddles and downed branches. They passed the turnoff to Harry's school. Hannah looked longingly down the pot-holed dirt road, but she couldn't see the yellow schoolhouse.

They'd chosen to visit the Hartes in the early evening in the hopes that, after a hearty midday meal and plenty of wine, the Reverend and his wife might be amenable to the idea of a sale. Rebekah noted that the opposite could also be true, that some who indulged would get nastier instead of more at ease. Hannah bet that Agnes Harte would be the former.

The sun was setting as Aaron and Hannah stepped up to the Hartes' front door. Aaron took off his hat and pulled the bell-cord. In the moments after the echo, Aaron looked long and hard at Hannah, who tried not to cringe under the ferocity of his gaze. He reached out and gripped her hand with his sea-calloused one.

"I'm proud of you, niece. I don't think I've ever been more proud."

As the door swung open, Aaron dropped her hand and stepped forward.

Hannah had hoped Bintu would answer so she could give her friend a warning of their intentions, but it wasn't. It was a small boy of about eight, another house slave in the Hartes' retinue. Hannah studied him to see if she knew him, but the boy hadn't been one of Harry's students when Hannah had been there.

The boy silently let them in. It was dark inside the house, darker than the thunderheads glowering outside. The boy gestured for them to stay where they were and disappeared under an arch.

In a few moments, the boy silently reappeared and beckoned to them. They followed under the archway, up the stairs, and down a short hallway, entering a room on the left. A parlor or drawing room, the only light in the room was a series of candles scattered on the various surfaces with elegant, expensive hurricane lamps over them. Damask curtains were drawn over the windows. An entire wall was an elaborate bookcase meant to shriek wealth and power. This room's intention was to intimidate.

Hannah crinkled her nose as she stepped into the room behind her uncle, struck by an overpoweringly sweet scent. In front of the doorway sat a long, wooden table with a huge vase of tea-roses, heads drooping sadly in the stuffy room. Puddles of petals clustered around the base of the vase.

Behind the table stood an ornate settee covered with dark material. Hulking shapes of furniture were scattered about and, as the boy led them around the table and settee, Hannah could make out a harpsichord in the corner. The room smelled like tea-roses mostly, but under that, there was a hint of decay, like a cat had left a dead offering hidden somewhere in the room. It was the most opulent room Hannah had ever seen, and the most oppressive.

The hearth was set into the far wall, dark and dead as the rest of the room, but there was still a heat screen set up in front of it, shielding the occupant of a dainty stool from imaginary flames. Perched there, staring intently at a white round of needlework, was Mistress Agnes Harte. Her voluminous skirts spilled over the stool and down to the ground, the white lace glowing in the darkness. Hannah and Aaron were standing in front of the settee, waiting for her to acknowledge them. Mistress Harte continued studying her needlework, her bent head exposing the severe part in her light hair, the pink skin of her scalp stretched mercilessly.

Finally, she looked up with a slight smile and knowing eyes. She had wanted them to wait. She motioned for them to sit, and it was only when they did, the settee issuing a sharp wooden shriek, that Hannah noticed the figure beside Mistress Harte, hunkered down on an ottoman, knees drawn up, with a sewing basket perched on top of them.

Hannah's insides turned to water. It was Bintu, but it wasn't Bintu. Hannah took in the details: hollowed cheeks, downcast eyes, loose sackcloth dress. This was Chastity, the Hartes' house girl. She hadn't even turned to see who had entered the room, just stayed rooted to the spot like another piece of furniture.

"Well, Master Lopez," Mistress Harte said, breaking the awkward silence. She handed her sewing round off to Bintu without looking at her. "To what do I owe this enormous pleasure?" The way she drew out the word *enormous* let Hannah know that Mistress Harte thought the opposite. "And this is your niece, I believe? Hannah, isn't it?"

At the mention of Hannah's name, Bintu's face twitched, and she jerked her head toward the settee, blue eyes meeting Hannah's for just a moment and then, as quick as a hummingbird, darting away again. Hannah's insides felt like a bucket of icy water had been dumped into them. Even Bintu's eyes were dead. Chastity, Hannah thought. She must remember to call her Chastity.

"Mistress Harte, I apologize for dropping in on you," Aaron began. "It was not my intention to intrude on you."

Mistress Harte's expression softened under Aaron's formality. "It doesn't put me out in the least," she said, turning on her stool to smile at them. "But I'm afraid you've missed Reverend Harte. He's off on a visit to a sick parishioner." The woman's face hardened again as she said this, and Hannah wondered if that was a lie. She was fairly certain that it was.

"Malachi," Mistress Harte said to the boy standing by a doorway. Hannah had completely forgotten that he was there. "Go tell Nan to bring—" She paused. "What shall you have for refreshment? Lemonade?"

"Lemonade is fine for me," Aaron said.

Mistress Harte turned her hard eyes on Hannah. "And you, dear?" The way she said that final word let Hannah know that she meant just the opposite.

"Yes, please."

Mistress Harte nodded at Malachi, who disappeared through the doorway.

"Now," Mistress Harte said, placing two fists on top of her knees. "Whatever can I do for you this evening?"

Aaron cleared his throat. "As you know, these two girls know each other."

Mistress Harte's face immediately changed. Her head cocked down so that she was looking up at the two of them, and her eyebrows raised into peaks. She looked, for a brief moment, like a fox who had just realized that the hen house door was wide open. "Who, your niece and my house servant? Chastity? Yes, I suppose they do." The fists that were propped on her knees tightened, clutching the fabric of her dress. She still held her sewing needle clenched in one fist like a tiny sword. "Why is this of any import to you, might I ask?"

"We have need of someone as bright as your girl. At the store. Cardozo's. You know it?"

"Of course, I know it," Mistress Harte snapped. The hand not holding her sewing needle smoothed the fabric of her dress, over and over. "Why ever would you have need of such a useless girl as this one?"

Malachi entered at that moment with a tray and pitcher almost larger than he was. He put it carefully down, without bobbling it, blocking Mistress Harte from view for a moment. Hannah tried to catch Bintu's eye. Although she hadn't moved, Hannah could sense that Bintu's nerves were clenched as tightly as Mistress Harte's fists. They all remained silent while Malachi poured out three glasses. When he'd finished, Mistress Harte told him to be on his way. When she looked back at them, she looked less like a fox now, and more like a snake.

Aaron and Mistress Harte picked up their glasses to take a sip, and Aaron jabbed Hannah in the ribs with his elbow until she did the same. She sputtered and choked down a sip of the overly bitter liquid.

"So," Agnes asked after an awkward pause. "You are calling on me to ask to hire out one of my slave girls."

"It's not an uncommon practice to rent out slaves from one house to another," Aaron clarified.

"Well, it may be common practice in some households, but not this one," Mistress Harte simpered, placing her glass down on a crocheted coaster. "I will not rent out my property. And why would you want Chastity? She is the worst house slave we have. Very impudent and unmannerly."

"Actually, we were calling to ask you about buying her outright, if renting her was not an option. My niece has mentioned that your girl is an excellent seamstress and we have more work than we can manage. Chastity's ability with a needle would be a great asset to our business."

"Is that so?" Agnes Harte turned her head slowly toward the girl sitting at her feet, like a viper registering movement in the grass.

Even though Bintu hadn't outwardly moved, Hannah could feel her cringe.

"I heard she's almost as good as my sister," Aaron continued, leaning forward. Something had changed in the room, like the air pressure or another invisible element. Hannah knew Bintu felt it as well, but Uncle Aaron seemed to be verbally striding on, unaware of Mistress Harte's darkening visage.

"Is that so," Agnes Harte said again.

Hannah was suddenly overwhelmed with the feeling that, whatever Uncle Aaron planned on saying next, he should not.

"Yes," he said, as if he were closing a sale on a shipload of goods. "She could boost our business immensely, and with her improved English, be able to work closely with customers." He faltered on the final words as he saw the change in Mistress Harte's face.

"Work with customers, will she?" Mistress Harte said in a sing-song voice. "Improved English?" She turned toward Bintu. "Is this true, Chastity? Are you particularly adept with a needle?"

Bintu shook her head, only once, and then froze again, hands locked onto the sewing basket's handles. She realized her mistake, but only too late. Mistress Harte's mouth curved into a sickle-shaped smile.

"Are you calling this man a liar, Chastity?" Mistress Harte's head swiveled on a long boneless neck, looking from Aaron to Bintu. "Is that *so?*"

On the last word, Agnes Harte's hand struck, quick as a serpent, jabbing the sewing needle into Bintu's leg directly above her kneecap. Hannah jerked and her breath seized in her throat like a fishhook. Then Mistress Harte's hand was perched back on her knee, fist still brandishing its tiny sword. It was almost as if it hadn't happened, it was so fast.

On Bintu's leg, a tiny flower of blood bloomed on the sackcloth where the needle had plunged in. Bintu had not moved a muscle or cried out. Hannah was staring at her friend, completely at a loss as to what to do or say, her own righteous fire extinguished with that needle jab.

"No, Mistress," Bintu breathed, still looking at the far wall, not at them, eyes trained on the hulk of a harpsichord in the corner. "I am not calling this gentleman a liar."

Hannah couldn't believe how calm Bintu remained, whereas Hannah felt like screaming, and her muscles were so tense that she was hovering over the settee.

"Well, then, you admit," hissed Mistress Harte, "you are exceptionally *quick* and *clever.*"

On both *quick* and *clever*, Agnes Harte stabbed with her needle again in the same spot she'd struck before. Now there were three blood-blossoms tattooing Bintu's dress.

Aaron put his hand out, perhaps to stop Mistress Harte, but she looked at him with such reproach that he froze, hand hovering above the lemonade pitcher. "Madam, I must recant. I in no way wanted to upset you."

Mistress Harte sat back on her stool, swept away in a gale of girlish giggles. "Dear Master Lopez," she said when she'd recovered, "I'm not upset." Her face turned sly again; Hannah fully expected a forked tongue to dart out from between her lips. "I am merely making a *point.*" Another stab to Bintu's leg, this one so hard that Bintu rocked away from her, her foot sliding halfway into the hearth.

Hannah's stomach clenched, and she felt as if she was going to vomit up all the bitter lemonade onto Mistress Harte's lovely rug. This display of cruelty was too much. For the rest of her days, she promised herself, she would fight this type of cruelty until she couldn't fight any longer.

"Point made," Aaron said shortly. "Let me ask you something, Mistress Harte. I can see that you are not amenable to the sale of your house girl," Aaron's hand tapped Hannah's back, just below the nape of her neck, three times—their signal. He would distract Mistress Harte while she handed off the note. But how? Bintu was wedged between the dead hearth and Mistress Harte herself. "I have another offer to make to you."

Mistress Harte said nothing, her face emotionless, but her fist trembled, still holding the needle, blood smeared down its shaft. Hannah fumbled under her apron for the pouch that held the folded note, extracting it and cupping it in her palm.

"Your harpsichord," he said, standing and gesturing toward the corner. "I wonder if I might examine it. It's an original—" He trailed off, waiting for Mistress Harte to supply the end of the sentence.

"An original Kirkman." Mistress Harte stood and dropped the needle into the sewing basket on Bintu's lap. She then brushed her hands together as if to rid them of something and picked up the candle on the side table. "Brought over from England." She walked toward the harpsichord, swatting Bintu in the face with her skirt as she passed.

Hannah's heart raced. *This is it!* She had to do it at this moment or Mistress Harte would see.

Aaron followed Mistress Harte, effectively making his body a barrier between the woman and the girls.

"Some like Shudi's instruments, but I think the Kirkman is far superior," Mistress Harte went on, setting her candle on the body of the instrument.

"Psst," Hannah hissed at her friend.

Bintu turned. Hannah glanced over at the pair by the harpsichord and then held out the note to her friend, mouthing, "Take it," across the table. Bintu shook her head and then turned her head away again. Hannah was flabbergasted. *What's she doing? Why won't she take it?*

"But I'm afraid Reverend Harte won't part with it," Mistress Harte was saying in the corner.

"Psst," Hannah tried again.

"It was given to him by his brother on our wedding day."

If Bintu wouldn't take the note it probably meant she'd made up her mind. Or perhaps she was too scared to take it, knowing what Mistress Harte might do to her. Hannah's mind raced for a way to get the note to her friend without putting her in danger. She bit her lower lip.

Mistress Harte was turning back toward them. Uncle Aaron's body still blocked her from view, but it would only be another second, and then Mistress Harte would be back by Bintu's side.

Just as Mistress Harte reached over to pick up her candle off the harpsichord, Hannah tried one last time.

"Pssst!" she hissed. Bintu's head turned imperceptibly, and her eyes locked with Hannah's. Hannah opened her hand, clearly showing the triangular folded note she had cupped there. Then she shoved her hand with the note underneath the cushion of the settee. Bintu's eyes watched her hand tuck the note under the cushion, and then her gaze snapped up.

Suddenly Mistress Harte loomed over her. Had she seen? Was she going to strike Hannah too? For many long moments, Hannah listened to the pulse banging in her ears. Finally, just as Hannah could almost feel the heat of the woman's palm against her cheek, Mistress Harte swished by Hannah and made her way to the parlor door, the heady scent of tea-roses trailing after her.

"Neither my house girl nor my harpsichord is for sale or rent. Now, I'm afraid our visit is at an end. I've tired of your company."

Hannah stood and followed Uncle Aaron toward the door. Bintu stayed where she was.

As they exited the parlor into the dim hallway, Aaron made a slight bow toward their hostess.

"Thank you, Mistress Harte, for your excellent company and the lemonade. It was very enlightening."

Hannah surprised herself by giving Mistress Harte a small but steady curtsey and then she hurried after Malachi leading her uncle down the stairs. They stepped onto the Hartes' broad porch as the front door shut and the latch went home with a *clack*. A huge weight ran off Hannah's shoulders as they walked down the steps toward the cobblestone, leaving her nauseated.

"Did you do it?" Aaron murmured when they were halfway down the path.

"Kind of. She wouldn't take it, so I stuffed it under a cushion. She saw me do it."

Aaron put a hand on Hannah's shoulder. "Well, we tried. And you weren't wrong, Hannah. That woman has it in for that poor girl. Did you see her with the needle?"

Hannah nodded, the sick feeling surging up her throat, burning it sour.

"Now we wait to see if the girl will give us a sign, or burn the note up in the kitchen fire."

"Maybe she'll leave it to collect dust like the rest of the furniture in that horrid room."

"We'll have to wait and see. It was pretty horrid, wasn't it?"

The night was gathering itself on the horizon, dyeing everything indigo.

The two walked around the back of the house, keeping to the far perimeter of the yard. They found a spot across the service road next to the back of the Hartes' house and seated themselves on a rock wall under a willow, the trailing branches shrouding them in darkness.

"Now we wait and see," Aaron said.

CHAPTER 21

Dusk came down around them. Hannah and Aaron folded into the shadows beneath the willow tree, unmoving, unspeaking, both stewing in silence at what they'd witnessed. It was darker on the inside of the tree than it was on the outside, like a cocoon of black feathers. The rustling leaves whispered all around them.

After several moments, Hannah spoke up. "Did you see Mistress Harte's face when she spoke of her husband?"

"I did. What of it?"

"I thought she was lying about his being away to visit a sick parishioner."

"I think she was lying as well."

"Why?"

"Well, Reverend Harte is known to have a roving eye. It's part of the reason why that woman is so bitter. I assumed when she said he was off visiting a sick parishioner, what she meant was that he was off gallivanting with someone else. Someone female. Who isn't his wife."

"I could tell she was lying. Also, when she called me *dear* and said it was an *enormous pleasure* to see us. All tomfoolery."

Aaron was silent for many minutes, startling Hannah when he resumed speaking.

"It's part, I think, of why she's so cruel to Bintu."

"What do you mean?"

"There was a slave in Brazil I heard of on one of my journeys. Your friend there reminds me of her. It's part of the reason I've agreed to help her. I've seen how these things end. It's rarely good for anyone involved, and almost never for the slave."

"How does Bintu remind you of the Brazilian slave?"

"Her eyes, mostly. The slave in Brazil, Escrava Anastacia, she's famous now. She also had blue eyes and black skin. She was also very beautiful. That's what got her into trouble."

"What happened to her?"

"She was made to wear an iron mask at all times, over her mouth mostly, so she couldn't speak. All because her master's son had fallen in love with her. When the sailors speak of the blue-eyed slave, it is not of her beauty but of her misfortune. I feel that, with Reverend Harte's wandering eye, it is only a matter of time before it falls on Bintu."

An iron mask! Hannah could easily see Mistress Harte creating some sort of torture device for Bintu.

"What you said about justice—*Tzedek—*" Aaron's face was taut with emotion, "—I know in my heart that what Mistress Harte is doing in there is not right or just. And since I know, I must do something about it. Before it's too late."

After what felt like almost an hour, the church bells at St. Michael's in the center of town bonged once, signaling it was half past eight. Beside her, Uncle Aaron uncrossed his legs and pulled the willow twig out of his mouth.

"Look," he said, moving to the edge of their leafy enclosure. Hannah stepped up next to him and pushed aside the curtain of leaves. The Harte house was beginning to glow in the darkness. Windows on the first and second floors pulsed orange like amber as lamps and candles were lit inside. The third-floor room, with only one window set just under the eaves, stayed black.

"Let's see what the girl will decide," Aaron murmured.

Hannah stared so hard at the house that her vision began to tunnel. She willed Bintu to give them the sign, the sign that she agreed to take her chances away from the Hartes. Hannah couldn't stand the idea of Bintu spending the rest of her life as Chastity, growing old next to that dead hearth while Reverend Harte leered at her and Mistress Harte inflicted a thousand tiny cuts until she bled to death.

People were moving in the rooms, shadows thrown up against the curtains. The kitchen door swung open, spilling a path of bright light almost all the way to their tree. The cook threw a pan full of hot water across the yard, and then swung the door shut. The puddle steamed.

Most of the lighted windows were on the ground floor. The second floor had only two windows that glowed with lamplight and the crucial window on the third floor, the only one that mattered to them, stayed dark.

"Look, there!" Aaron grabbed Hannah's forearm.

In one window on the second floor, perhaps the window to a hallway, a lamp bobbed along like an especially steady firefly. It floated along, grew increasingly brighter, and then disappeared.

Hannah sagged and Aaron let out a low whistle of disappointment. They watched the upper floors of the Harte house for a few more minutes, spying only darkness.

"Well, that's it then," he said, letting the leafy curtain fall back and slapping his hat against his thigh. "She's made her choice. We said we'd wait until eight, it's half past that now. We've waited long enough. Time to go." A peal of thunder rolled across the sky, and on the tail end of it, Hannah thought she heard people shouting.

Aaron pushed his way through the tree close to the rock wall to avoid detection. Hannah was rooted to the spot, clinging to the willow branches near her. She couldn't believe that Bintu hadn't given them the sign, deciding not to take the risk to steal her freedom.

"Hannah," Aaron said from outside the willow's penumbra. When Hannah looked over her shoulder at him, all she could see of him were his leather boots. "It's done. Let's go."

"Come on, Bintu. *Please*," she whispered, and waited for another minute, then sighed and hung her head. She turned and pushed her way through the branches, following her uncle. A bramble snagged her skirt, and she had to stop to pull it free. When she did, she glanced at the Harte house one last time. A moment ago, it had looked like an ornate cake, with glowing second floor windows as candle toppers. *Now it looks more like a ship sailing through the darkness*, Hannah thought. She jerked her dress free and the hem ripped. She sighed. Her mother was not going to like that. She pushed the rest of her way through the hanging willow branches.

She took three steps and then stopped, spun, and stared hard at the house. A ship? With anchor lights? Why would she think that? It *did* look like a ship with anchor lights now, because there was a light at the very top. "Look," she said, pointing.

Aaron stopped walking down the lane and turned back to look at the house. He studied it for a few and then whistled again. "Well, I'll be damned."

There, in the tiny window under the eaves on the third floor was a small candle, beaming in the darkness. The sign.

CHAPTER 22

I t was way too bright to be scurrying around doing such dastardly
deeds. This sort of undertaking needed to be executed at night, or
at least during a fierce storm. To Hannah's dismay, the day dawned
positively balmy. The sun warmed her back and her dark hair through
her bonnet as she made her way through the warren of streets to the
predetermined meeting place. The whole way there, Hannah was
mentally wringing her hands. *Will Bintu show up?*

It had been decided that Hannah would lead Bintu down to the
docks where she would meet Uncle Aaron. He would have the girl
pose as a slave he was taking with him on a voyage north.

It was agreed that if the girls were stopped on their way to the
wharves, Hannah could drop her uncle's name. The name Lopez
opened many doors in this town and probably would get them out
of trouble. Bintu would have her slave badge, but she still might raise
suspicions regardless of the sliver of metal pinned to her chest.

As Hannah approached the corner of Bedon's Alley and Church
Street, her heart was in her throat. The town was surprisingly quiet

for this time of day, just after lunch. It reminded Hannah eerily of the slave auction where she'd first encountered Bintu. This close to the center of town, the houses were densely packed. The smell and tickle of horses and sawdust diluted the tang from the Ashley and Cooper, twin rivers embracing Charles Town on either side. She slowed at the corner that Hannah had lettered onto her note to Bintu.

A figure approached from an adjacent street, a figure with a full skirt and a head topped with a straw bonnet just like Hannah's, bowed so it made it difficult to see her face. Hannah's heart leapt as the figure reached the corner, but then the woman kept going on her determined route and crossed the street.

Hannah sighed, and stepped into the road, looking for wagons or horses, and hurried over to their corner. *Where's Bintu? Did she change her mind and decide not to come?* Hannah had timed it perfectly. As she stepped up onto the curb, the church bell struck three, the jangle of the new church bells jarring her nerves but also telling her that she was on schedule.

But where is Bintu? Hannah's breath hitched and she pushed a sob down. She couldn't cry here, on the street. She felt that Bintu had betrayed *her*, even if she did it for her own survival. Or that's what she tried to remind herself as Hannah waited on the corner, fingering the frayed ribbon from her bonnet that trailed down her bodice. She reminded herself that Bintu had to make her own decision; Hannah couldn't make it for her. *And besides, maybe she's just late.*

Minutes felt like hours. The more she waited, the more the thick wad of tears pushed themselves up her throat. She was just about to leave, most likely sobbing, when she felt a tug on her sleeve. She turned, and there, smiling into her face under a broad bonnet, was Bintu.

"Hello," Hannah said astonished. "It's you, here you are."

"Here I am."

After a few moments, she pulled Bintu into a fierce hug. "Are you all right?" she whispered into Bintu's ear. The girl nodded against her shoulder.

They stood back and Hannah held Bintu at arm's length, studying her. "Good, I was very worried. I was downright scared for you. That Mistress Harte, she's . . . she's . . . "

"Awful. She's so awful," Bintu finished in a whisper, keeping her bonnet down. "She's even worse of late. With the Reverend gone for such long hours, she's very frantic."

The girls began to walk, arms woven and steps in sync. Heads bowed, they followed the narrow cart road between the smaller yet still distinguished houses of Charles Town's middle gentry. They aimed their hushed conversation at their feet as they walked swiftly along and let their straw bonnets block their faces.

"We're going down to the wharves. To meet Uncle Aaron," Hannah said. "You'll be traveling with him as his slave who will be given to his family up north."

Bintu hung onto Hannah's forearm, holding them back. Hannah turned toward her, a quizzical look on her face. Bintu looked at her, saying nothing, but with the same mute horror that Hannah had seen in the Hartes' drawing room.

"You've nothing to worry about with Uncle Aaron," Hannah said, tugging her along. "I promise. You're safe with him."

The girls made their way down Gadsen's Alley, a narrow lane that could more accurately be called a footpath. An iron fence ran alongside, with ornate swirls and gargoyles and roses wound around the black spokes. Thorny branches poked through the fence and grabbed at the girls' skirts as they swished by.

"I knew why you were there, when I saw you in the drawing room," said Bintu. "The moment I heard your voice I knew why you were there, but I couldn't say a thing, not even to show you I knew you were there."

"Awful. Is your leg okay?"

Bintu nodded, jaw clenched. Hannah hadn't noticed a limp or any other telltale sign of abuse, but she imagined Bintu was good at hiding her injuries these days.

"It's all right. I'm all right. Now. I'm just relieved she didn't get the satisfaction of hurting me worse. Like she'd wanted." There was something brittle in Bintu's voice, a tone Hannah had never heard before. "I'm sure the Reverend would have seen it as a great loss if she killed me, but the Mistress would've done it anyway. Just to spite him."

Now they were walking between several back kitchen gardens of Charles Town's grander homes, closing in on the wharves. A murmur welled up from somewhere; Hannah hoped it wasn't another auction at the wharves, which would make Bintu's departure even more conspicuous.

As they walked in silence, Hannah felt a chasm yawning between them. She could never know what Bintu had been through, how she felt, no matter what Hannah did or how much she wanted to empathize. It was astonishing that they were so close yet had experienced such different lives thus far. Hannah couldn't imagine living with someone who tortured her, like Mistress Harte had tortured Bintu, and actually being owned by her tormentor.

Hannah's grandmother had told her stories about the Inquisition back in the old country, how scared the Jewish people were of persecution, of the knock on the door in the middle of the night, of the unannounced visitor. Perhaps her grandmother would've understood Bintu better than Hannah. Maybe Hannah and Levi were the first generation in a long while that could breathe without constantly fearing for their lives or their freedom. It was a feeling, her Avo always said, that they shouldn't forget, lest history repeat itself.

Bintu and Hannah arrived at the spot where their little lane crossed a larger thoroughfare and turned into Chalmers Alley. She had promised her mother that they would pick their way to the docks using only back paths to avoid any untoward attention. At the place where their small footpath blended into the larger road, Hannah paused and, holding on to the brim of her bonnet, looked one way and then another, making sure that there were no carts bearing down on them.

The girls scurried across the road like field mice across a wagon path and started on the narrower, shadowed lane again. The day instantly grew darker as soon as the houses and broad-branched trees loomed over them. They once again had to squeeze to fit two abreast, but neither girl seemed to want to drop the other's hand.

"Hannah," Bintu said from beside her. "Thank you."

Hannah took a step over a pile of horse chips. "For what?" she asked. The murmur of voices swelled, perhaps from a street market or a church celebration.

"For everything," Bintu said in a small voice. "For a chance at freedom, and a chance for my life. Thank you, Hannah."

Hannah was struck into silence. She could feel Bintu's awkward stiffness beside her, so she forced herself to respond out of the swirling well of happiness and fear. "It was nothing," she stuttered. "Anyone would've done it."

Bintu halted, stopping Hannah as well. Hannah turned to look at her friend. Bintu didn't speak until she had Hannah's full attention.

"That's not true," Bintu said, her strong chin jutting out from the oval of her bonnet. "It isn't nothing . . . it's everything. And not everyone would do it, you know that, and I know that. What you've done, what you're doing, Hannah, it's a very special thing. And that's because you're a special person. I want you to know how much it means to me."

Hannah's vision filled with tears. "You're welcome," she said at last as tears swelled in Bintu's ice-blue eyes. "You're welcome, Bintu. I need to thank you too, for teaching me. About friendship, and loyalty. And about *Tzedek*."

The girls squeezed one another's hands, and then they started on their way again.

Fifteen minutes later, Bintu and Hannah were at the end of their path. Here they picked up the final alley to the water. The smell of silt and mud permeated the already thick air as they crossed Union Street together and darted down the last dark path, Unity Alley, that was so narrow it could not accommodate both of them abreast. Bintu was first, and Hannah walked close behind. Their broad-brimmed bonnets blocked their view of everything else as they stepped over roots, horse chips, and brambles. Passing one back garden, a dog lunged and snapped at the girls, forcing breathy shrieks from both. They giggled nervously at their own fear as they hurried past the tethered beast.

Through the murmuring of a crowd from afar, the girls could now discern shouts of "Liberty!" and the crackle and smell of burning, and the occasional tinkle of shattered glass. Hannah hoped against hope that whatever was happening, it wasn't happening down by the harbor. It never occurred to her that whatever was happening was moving.

Hannah had her eyes locked on Bintu's back, lightly holding a fold of her dress as they tripped down the narrow path. She tugged and Bintu slowed, turning toward her.

"Bintu, do you hear that? Like the sound of a crowd?"

Hannah could now see the end of the alleyway, past Bintu, where it opened onto East Bay. There were people quickly striding past the mouth of the alley, not merely walking or meandering. A lot of people. The purposeful way they strode set Hannah's heart fluttering. Something was happening.

One man with a red face and brown breeches was carrying a flag with red and white alternating stripes, snapping and furling out behind him as he walked past.

Hannah suddenly realized what she was looking at. It was not a mid-afternoon crowd; it was a mob. A large wooden structure that looked vaguely like a person was borne by on the shoulders of the marching men. And then, in quick succession, it was followed by what looked like a large black box. A coffin, Hannah realized. A giant coffin. Her tongue felt like a horse blanket, hairy and coarse.

The smashing of glass no longer seemed accidental, but malicious. The smell wasn't the cookfires and blacksmiths' forges that she was used to. Sure enough, men with oily torches strode by the end of Unity Alley, one turning and beckoning to someone behind him before running off after the effigy and its coffin.

"We can't go down there," Hannah whispered. Fear made her mouth dry.

"Oh no," Bintu breathed, staring at something beyond Hannah's shoulder. Hannah whipped her head around. Down at the other end of the pathway overhung with brambles, a man in a tricorn hat was striding toward them. He too looked as if he had a definitive purpose. And he was staring only at them.

To Hannah, it felt like stepping into a puddle that only looks ankle-deep but turns out to be knee high. She swayed on her feet. Bintu's fingers were talons on her arm, holding her up. Hannah knew who that man was; she'd seen him the other night, in a portrait hung up in Mistress Harte's hallway.

It was Reverend Horace Harte, and he was coming right at them.

The girls took two steps back toward the mouth of the alley.

"We have to go," Bintu said, the pupils in her wide blue eyes pinpricks in terror.

"We can't! That's a mob! And they look mad!"

"You don't understand. He can't catch me. He can't!"

She suddenly spurted off down the alley, toward the crowd.

"No! Bintu!" Hannah shrieked and took off after her.

"You! Girl!" came a shout from behind them. "Chastity! Halt!"

Each word sounded angrier than the last, like a *blat* from a furious waterfowl. The girls bolted down the narrowing pathway until they could brush their fingers along the painted brick walls. Hannah had her hand on Bintu's back, stealing quick glances over her shoulder as they ran, trying to keep her mental map of Charles Town straight in her head.

Reverend Harte was gaining on them, his knee-high black boots pumping up and down as he ran, coattails flying out behind, looking all the more like a furious black goose.

The girls paused at the mouth of the alley, teetering on the edge of the crowd for a few seconds. The throng packed the main thoroughfare of East Bay Street, a wide promenade that ran parallel to the wharves.

It was a motley tough lot—working men, vagabonds, and sailors dressed in cotton shirts and breeches with some wearing waistcoats and some in leather vests and for the most part all drunk. They were red-faced and shouting, mouths wide, faces sweaty, eyebrows clenched, mad. They marched past the two frozen girls, bootheels kicking up clouds of dust, a cacophony of voices and feet stamping and chanting drowning out everything else. The stench of urine and strong liquor and spent torches rolled over them and Hannah gagged. Bintu chanced a glimpse behind them and shrieked, plunging into the crowd and dragging Hannah by the arm.

Hannah looked back and caught a glimpse of Reverend Harte's furious face, only ten feet away, bright red patches standing out clearly on his milk-white skin as he lunged for them, and then she was enveloped into the crowd. It was like being overwhelmed by a herd of drunk horses. Everywhere there were men's arms and elbows and knees and marching boots and yelling mouths, jostling and stamping and jabbing them. She could barely keep a hold on Bintu's forearm, as they hop-skipped along with the flow of the mob. They couldn't help but move, for if they stopped, they would be ground underfoot and pummeled into the dust beneath the crowd's boots.

The men shouted, "Liberty! Liberty!" throwing their fists in the air. The man next to Bintu was naked from the waist up and sweat coursed over his blotchy hairy back. Bintu stared at Hannah, eyes huge in the shadow of her bonnet.

Hannah skipped and ran along, trying with all her might not to trip on the edge of her dress or run into the man in front of her. Her bonnet, which protected her from the scrutinizing gaze of the throng, also made it very difficult to keep her feet under her or see what was going on. She stared down at the cobblestones and clung to Bintu's arm like a limpet as she ran as best she could.

Hannah felt like they'd been running among the smelly, loud men forever. As they were buoyed along in the filthy crowd, almost held up by the large men's elbows and borne along like the effigy, she darted glances up at the buildings above their heads. She could barely see the eaves of the building they passed. These men were all so tall, they almost blocked out the sky itself.

It might have been a half hour, or it might've been more than an hour, Hannah couldn't tell. The roar of the crowd kept her from hearing St. Michael's bells, chiming the time.

At some point, she felt a sharp yank on her arm and looked over just in time to catch Bintu's elbow as the girl fell forward. She dragged her friend up, holding fast as she kept her feet, so Bintu wouldn't take them both under.

Just when Hannah thought she couldn't take any more, that she should just stop running and let these strange men flatten her into the horse dung and cobblestones, the throng began to slow. She decreased her gait from a hard trot to a walk and tried to catch her breath. When her heart slowed from its triple-hammer beat, she looked up. Above the heads and hats rose masts, spiking into the sky behind them. Hannah could just hear the slap of the halyards against the wooden masts in the lull of the crowd's buzz.

It seemed as if they'd made it to the wharves after all.

There was something happening toward the front, but for the life of them the girls couldn't see it, no matter how they craned their necks. The men around them still hadn't fully realized the girls were in their midst, so intent they were on what was going on in front.

Despite her painful exhausted feet, Hannah was curious. *What are they doing up there?*

A roar boomed from the crowd and, above the men's heads, a large pole with a cross bar jutting from it sprung up at an angle and then straightened triumphantly.

"What is that?" Bintu whispered as they clutched each other, cowering, like field mice taking cover under a bush in a thunderstorm.

A rope was thrown over the crossbar and pulled up, revealing a noose, and the men around them hollered and cheered.

"That," Hannah replied, "is a gallows."

CHAPTER 23

A weird hush fell over the crowd of jostling sweaty men. Hannah looked around, pulling her bonnet this way and that to take it all in, but she couldn't spot another female or child in their midst. The whole crowd seemed to be made up of drunken, red-faced, sweaty, angry men.

A hush grew into a silence throbbing with expectancy, like the sea marsh just before a storm blew in from the river. A few of the men around them looked down with surprise at the two girls huddled together, but no one asked them what they were doing there. They just turned back to whatever was going on up front.

The girls could barely see the gallows and the men's arms working it. Setting up a series of ropes and pulleys, the same that they used yards away in the shipyard, the men hauled on their end of the rope to the encouraging chants of "Liberty!" and "Damn the Stamp Act!"

Slowly, foot by foot, the top of the effigy came into view, the noose around its neck yanking it up to hang from the crossbar. It dangled obscenely, its large, outsized head and painted-on eyes seeming to accuse each of them with its gaze. It was dressed in clothing and a pinned label on its lapel read *Stamp Collector.*

So here it is, Hannah thought. *Here's the spark, and our town a tinderbox. Just like Uncle Aaron said.*

Thinking of Uncle Aaron jolted Hannah out of her reverie, and she tugged on Bintu's sleeve.

"We've got to get out of here!"

"What about the Reverend? What if he's still looking for me?"

"We're going to have to take that chance. We can't stay here."

In the shadow of her bonnet's brim, Bintu set her lips and nodded. "All right, let's go."

Hannah tried a smile, and then the girls shouldered their way through the bristly forest of men. Hannah was in front, pulling Bintu along behind her. The farther they muscled their way in, the worse it smelled of sweat and drink and urine. They were shouts of "Down with the Stamp Act" and the like, as the two girls battled her way through the crowd. Soon, quite a few gruff voices called after them, shouting, "Hey Missy!" and "Hey, you there!" as hairy arms reached out to grab them as they darted out of reach.

The green-brown tint of the river and the brown of the piers glinted through the next row of men. They were almost through. Strength surged through the coiled springs of Hannah's legs as she pushed through the last line of human bodies to the freedom of the docks beyond. Suddenly, Bintu's hand was ripped from hers. She stumbled, and a hand clamped on her shoulder.

The hand roughly spun her around and she was face-to-face with the Reverend Harte, whose countenance was all one red blotch.

"You!" he hissed, fully transformed into the furious waterfowl she had imagined him as.

Hannah glanced around her, searching the crowd for Bintu, but she was gone.

"Where is she?" Reverend Harte snarled above the crowd's murmur, his tricorn hat askew, droplets of spittle spraying into

Hannah's eyes. She cringed, but he had her by both arms now and was shaking her like a bad puppy; each word he shouted in her face was punctuated by a violent shake. "Where is Chastity?"

Hannah's head was flopping back and forth so much she could hardly keep her balance, but it didn't matter as he had pulled her off the ground anyway. She tried to kick him, but she had no leverage as her boot only whiffed through the air. The Reverend looked down at her futile swinging foot and a mean smile came over his face.

"Do you have any idea what I am going to do to her if you don't tell me where she is, girl?" All desperation was out of his voice now. "I will brand her, and I will cut off her ear; that's a fact. No one runs away from Reverend Harte. And," he said, giving her another mean shake and setting her head bobbing, "I will make you watch."

She recoiled as far away as she could from his leering countenance, trying to get away from his yellowed teeth and bloodshot eyes. His breath was horrible and hot on her cheek, reeking of boiled vinegar and onions. He released one of her upper arms and her boots finally touched the cobblestones, and then he raised one hand high in the air, palm open. Hannah cringed, awaiting the blow.

Abruptly, from out of the crowd, Bintu darted forward between two men, stopping in front of the astonished reverend, his open palm frozen in surprise. Bintu glared up at him and yelled, *"Juso jawo!"* and then reared back, and punched him with all her might in the stomach.

The Reverend's eyes bulged and all of his breath *whuffed* out of him as he let Hannah abruptly go. There was a guffaw from the crowd of men around them. Hannah dropped hard onto her backside, hard enough to make her jaws clack together.

To everyone's utmost surprise, Bintu wasn't finished with Reverend Harte. *"Buubu fimfoo!"* she screamed, and reared back again and kicked him between the legs.

Reverend Harte could not get another breath in. His face went immediately yellow, like he'd been covered in candle wax, and then an unseemly grey as his eyes fluttered up into his head and he sank to his knees, hands crisscrossed in front of him.

Bintu seemed stunned at her own power as she stood over him and the Reverend slowly toppled over onto the cobblestones, wheezing.

It was at this moment the world snapped back into focus for Hannah. And simultaneously for the men around them who had finally taken notice of the young girls' presence. She heard a snicker from one side and a gruff mumble on the other. The men on the opposite side of the cleared space were looking at Bintu with fear, disgust, and hatred.

Hannah jumped up, grabbed Bintu by the arm, and yanked her along, shouldering through the men, and finally bursting through the exterior skin of the mob. Shouts of "Hey!" and "Wait!" followed them. She took off, heels clattering down the wooden dock, Bintu's pounding right behind hers.

She didn't dare look back, not even to check if Bintu was with her, until she zagged left onto Eveleigh's Wharf where her uncle's ship was docked at the far end. She leapt from plank to plank down the dock until she came to the small warehouse where cargo was stored as a ship was unloaded. She flung open the creaky old door and lunged into the dim interior that smelled like the combined cargo of hundreds of ships—spices and animal hides and old paper. A moment later, Bintu tumbled in behind her. Together they swung the door shut and slammed home a plank to lock it.

They stood there, panting furiously, hands on the door, dust motes and rope wisps cartwheeling in the air around them. When their breathing had slowed and a few moments had passed, they looked at one another.

"Well," Hannah said.

"Yes," Bintu agreed. "Well."

"You certainly showed him."

"Yes, I certainly did."

They sat down, backs against the door, listening for the tell-tale footsteps of pursuers outside.

"Bintu?" Hannah said after a few minutes of blessed silence. "What did you yell at him, before you kicked him? What language was that?"

"It was my language, of my home. Mandinka." Bintu looked slightly abashed. "The first time I called him a wicked, irresponsible person."

"And that second thing you yelled?"

"Well, that time I called him a baboon fart."

Hannah's eyes bulged and she burst out laughing, trying to muffle it with her hands, snorting and snuffling.

"Baboon fart?" she squeaked.

Bintu nodded, starting to chuckle herself. "Filthy baboon fart," she clarified, which set them both off into muffled guffaws.

When Hannah could speak again, she said, "Bintu?"

"Hmmm?"

"Remind me never to make you mad, all right?"

Bintu croaked out a laugh which grew into a maniacal giggle. The girls laughed as silently as they could, with manic snorts and chuffs, until tears streamed down their cheeks. When they could breathe again, Bintu placed her head on Hannah's shoulder.

"Yes," she said with great satisfaction. "It is not wise to make me mad."

CHAPTER 24

The two stayed huddled together on the floor, their backs against barrels and crates. Shafts of sunlight speared through the cracks in the wall, illuminating the dust dancing through the cramped space.

They could hear the not-so-distant throng of men, the pulsation of yells and jeers, none of them good-natured. Occasionally, and to the girls' utmost horror and hope, boot heels clomped down the pier. But so far no one, not even Uncle Aaron, had tried to open the door of the little warehouse.

After a while, Hannah asked Bintu, "What will you do when you are free?"

"I don't know. I want to go home. I want to see my family. I know medicine so maybe I can tend to sick people. Maybe I can sew things." She paused, looking down at her hands. "I want to go back across the ocean and see my mother."

"Oh, Bintu," Hannah said with a teary sigh, her exhaustion close to the surface. "I want that for you, too. So much." They were silent for a while. Then Hannah said, "Do you remember the part of the

Scripture that Harry was reading when Mistress Harte came? That made her so mad?"

Bintu shook her head.

"Harry was reading Exodus, the story of how the Jews were led out of slavery to the promised land. It says that when the seas parted and the Jewish people fled safely to freedom, Miriam took out her timbrel and led the women away, all singing praise. She was brave, like you, Bintu."

"Did she ever find it?"

"What?"

"Her freedom?"

"Yes, she did. Just like you will."

The girls lapsed into silence. Then, after what seemed like an eternity, a pair of boot heels clip-clopped down the pier, slowed, and then stopped just outside their door. The girls scooted closer together as they listened.

Then came the knock, three fast, then one long pause, and then two more quick ones. Hannah and Bintu let out their trapped breath, exhaling in unison, then stood up to remove the plank that locked the door from the inside. The door creaked inward on ancient hinges as a hooded head poked in. Hannah's heart spasmed. Slowly the figure swiveled, scanning the murky depths. It was almost twilight by now, the skies purple and luminescent, and there was little light in the warehouse by which to see. One curl of white hair sprung forth from beneath the hood.

"Say something!" came a low voice from the hooded depths. "Girls, are you there?"

Hannah's heart unclenched and blood surged through her limbs, making her fingers and feet tingle. It was him. "Yes! Uncle Aaron! Here we are!" Hannah stood and flung her arms around him with such force it almost bowled them back onto the dock again, in plain view of all.

Uncle Aaron squeezed her tight as he steadied them. Using one hand on the door frame, he stepped them inside and swung the door shut.

"Oh, my sweet niece, I am so glad to see you." He squeezed her once more, planting a kiss on the top of her sweaty head and then releasing her. "Hannah, we need to move quickly." Then, "Hello." Bintu bowed. "We are about to embark on quite a journey together. Are you ready for it?"

"I've never been more ready, Master Lopez."

"You understand the cost, though? The risk?"

Bintu nodded. "I would rather be dead than be a slave."

In the silence that followed this, the sound of the crowd came to them through the warehouse's thin walls, intensifying, swelling like a wave, cresting, and then dying down. Aaron whipped off his cloak and swung it around Bintu's shoulder in one lithe motion.

"The time is now or never. And you, sweet niece," he said in a mocking scold, but his eyes were deadly serious. "You stay right here without moving an inch until at least it is full dark. And then run you home, little field mouse. Straight back home."

Bintu straightened the cloak on her shoulders.

"You, girl." Bintu nodded, the floppy hood nodding emphatically with her.

"Keep those eyes of yours pointed at the deck if we see anyone," Aaron poked his head out of the warehouse. "They're like lighthouse beams, those," he remarked over his shoulder. "But blue."

With that he was out the door.

Hannah and Bintu faced one another, both realizing that this was their last moment together. They clumsily hugged one another, talking at once.

"Bintu, I—"

"Never can repay you—"

"How will I know you're safe?"

They both fell quiet.

"Well then," Hannah said.

"Well then," Bintu echoed. "Goodbye, my good, good friend."

"Goodbye," Hannah said faintly, and then Bintu was gone, pulling the hood close to her face and darting out.

Hannah was left alone in the musty warehouse with the scents of all corners of the world surrounding her.

After a few moments Hannah couldn't resist it and poked her head out of the little warehouse. She could still see Bintu and her Uncle Aaron at the far end of the pier, making their way to the last merchant ship on the portside. As Hannah sidled carefully out the doorway, the pair turned left and headed up the gangplank.

She crept along the side of the warehouse, weaving between barrels and piles of nets to peer around the corner, looking toward the base of the pier and the crowd of rowdy men. On the edge of the crowd closest to the wharves, and to Eveleigh Wharf in particular, was a tall man in black making his way down the wharf, scrutinizing each pier as he passed them. Hannah crouched back, heart hammering like a rabbit catching sight of the fox.

It was Reverend Harte again, and he was coming right toward her hiding place.

From her shelter on the lee side of the warehouse, she could clearly see Bintu and Uncle Aaron, shadowy figures silhouetted against the iridescent sunset. They were talking to a man with a captain's hat at the base of the gangplank. Hannah's heart skipped at breakneck speed. If they didn't get onto the ship this instant, Harte would see them for sure. He was only one pier down, at Vanderhorst's, craning his long stork neck around as he peered up its length.

"Come on, come on!" Hannah murmured, glancing back at her uncle and Bintu who hadn't moved. As she watched, Aaron gestured toward Bintu and the girl pulled her hood off, revealing her short dark hair. She still kept her eyes downcast, however.

Hannah gasped. *This is even worse!* To Hannah, Bintu was

instantly recognizable. *If Reverend Harte calls her name, even her Christianized slave name,* Hannah thought, *Bintu will whip her head around and those blue eyes will give her away.*

Hannah peered around the edge of the warehouse again and saw that the Reverend was fifteen feet away from where she hid. The carved lines on his face made him look sick, and his skin was pallid as an angry flush crept out of his collar. He turned his gaze toward their pier, and she flinched back around her corner, hoping against hope that Aaron and Bintu were safely aboard. But they weren't. They stood like figureheads, frozen on the plank.

Should she do something? Yell? Rush at Reverend Harte? Maybe she could push him into the river. As much as she would've liked to, she shrank from the idea. But what if it was for Bintu's freedom, and probably her life?

Hannah left the safety of the warehouse at her back and crept forward toward the base of the pier, crouching down behind three barrels just as Reverend Harte rounded toward the base of Eveleigh's pier. She bunched up her skirt, ready to pounce on the older man. Just as she was gathering her courage, leg muscles jittering, there was a massive *whoosh* in the atmosphere, a strange shift in pressure that made her eardrums momentarily clog up, followed by a cacophony of triumphant, drunken yells.

Behind the Reverend, the effigy had been lit, the flames eating up the dried corn husks inside it in an instant, the whole thing ablaze in a matter of seconds, pushing a wave of heat at them.

Hannah could feel the blast on her face even from thirty yards away. The Reverend was poised at the end of the dock, about to pivot and make his way up their pier to her hiding place, but, miraculously, the effigy had caught his attention, if only for a few moments. His head was turned in the opposite direction, watching the ugly scene on the market green.

Men's fists danced in the air in front of the burning effigy of the stamp collector. Hannah glanced back over her shoulder at the ship.

The light from the effigy lit up Bintu's face and, as their eyes met across the pier, Hannah realized her uncle was right. Those eyes were like blue lighthouse beams.

Aaron made a tight bow to the captain. The man saluted him and immediately turned back to the spectacle of the flaming effigy as Aaron hustled Bintu up the gangplank in front of him. She jumped onto the deck of the ship, flipped up the hood of her cloak, and trotted toward the stern, Aaron right behind her.

Hannah sagged with relief and turned back to the scene on the market green. The effigy was dying down, the flames licking up each side, bits of burning husk and cotton floating through the twilit air. Reverend Harte was turning back toward her hiding place, tricorn hat in hand. He wouldn't spot Bintu now; she was safe. Now it was only the two of them.

But, she realized with horror, she had missed her chance to escape him.

Then, as if another gift from the heavens, from somewhere in the mob came two musket shots and a torch cartwheeled through the air, smacking into the face of the effigy and letting out a shower of sparks as it bounced out of sight. The yells from the crowd swelled anew as the fire ate through the noose's rope and the effigy fell, arresting the Reverend's attention for a crucial thirty seconds.

Hannah's feet felt nailed to the dock, but somehow she roused them, fast walking up to Reverend Harte's back and slipping behind him, close enough to set the feather in his hat fluttering with her passing. She took five long strides away from him as casually as she could and then broke into a run. She couldn't help it. She sprinted away from the wharves, toward the warren of alleys leading through town. Her heart, for what seemed like the hundredth time that day, slammed painfully in her chest. She didn't dare look back. She felt his fingertips about to snatch her cloak and yank her backwards toward the angry mob of men and the horribly blackened burning thing at their center.

But his hand never fell.

When she reached the mouth of Longitude Lane, she scampered down the alley and stopped, back against the wall, panting fiercely from the exertion and pure terror. She expected the Reverend's shadow to eclipse the little ambient light that filtered through the maze of brush and branches clogging the mouth of the alley at any moment, but the light never dimmed.

In a few moments, she gathered what courage she had left to peek out of the snarl of thorns and blossoms. The wharves looked as chaotic as they had minutes before, with the surging throng of men and smoldering effigy against a deeper purpling sky.

Gathering her dusty skirt around her, she started trotting down the alley for home, picking up speed as she went. By the time she crossed King Street, oddly empty for this usually vibrant time of day, she was full out running, leaping over curbs and across mounds of horse droppings like a ballerina.

CHAPTER 25

It was almost dark by the time Hannah rounded the final corner and trotted up to the gate that led to the back garden of her house and their outdoor kitchen. She paused, hand on the latch, and peered through the snarl of vegetation toward the outdoor kitchen.

Usually the house would be dark, and Rebekah would be nodding off over her sewing. Not tonight. Through the whorls of dense vines and trees, Hannah could see that the outdoor hearth was still burning merrily, despite the fact that it was well after dinner.

She could hear someone, her mother she hoped, clanging utensils and the thump of crockery as it was placed indelicately on wood. Hannah took a deep breath, undid the latch, and pushed open the gate.

Rebekah stood next to the hearth, stirring a large pot with a long, brown-stained wooden spoon. Hannah stopped on the path and sniffed. Was her mother making apple butter at this time of night? Her brain couldn't quite comprehend what she was seeing.

For a moment, the whole ordeal of the mob and Reverend Harte drifted away on the scent of warm apples and sugar. Everything did, except for the absurd vision of her mother pouring ladleful after ladleful of grainy brown goop into the stoneware on the table in the little light that the lantern and a few candles provided. It was way too late for apple butter making. It was just so absurd.

Hannah couldn't help it. She was tired and emotionally exhausted, and she'd just lost the closest thing she'd ever had to a real friend. She giggled, and her mother glanced up. Laughter bubbled up at the sight of her mother's stained apron and bonnet askew on her salt-and-pepper curls. Rebekah dropped the ladle, and trotted toward Hannah, her skirt almost upending the stoneware jars as she went by.

"Oh thank God," Rebekah said as she swept Hannah into her arms. The hug was quick and fierce. "Are you all right? Aaron sent a message about what was happening at the wharf. Did anyone hurt you?" she asked, peering into her daughter's face.

Hannah's mirth drained away, and she was surprised to find herself on the verge of tears. She shook her head firmly, and Rebekah must've seen the girl's eyes brimming, because she grabbed her upper arm, still sore from Reverend Harte's murderous grip, and propelled her down the small path toward the kitchen area.

When they got to the table, Rebekah snatched up an apron. "Here," she said, flinging it at Hannah. "There's no time. Put this on."

Hannah nodded, astonished, and wrestled into the apron. When she popped her head through and tied it, she turned around.

"All right, Mama, I've put on the—"

Before Hannah could finish, Rebekah sliced through the air with a wooden spoon and an arc of brown butter juice splattered the pristine front of Hannah's apron like a knife strike.

"Mama," Hannah sputtered.

In response, Rebekah dipped one finger into the ladle she'd discarded on the table, drawing a smudge of apple butter down the side of Hannah's cheek.

Hannah tried to push her off, exasperated. "Mama, what are you doing? Will you please tell me?"

"There's no time!" her mother hissed, thrusting the wooden spoon in her daughter's hands, pushing her toward the hearth. "Stir, Hannah! Stand there and stir!"

Hannah dutifully dipped the wooden spoon in the dark bubbling mixture, a thousand questions darting through her head, and stirred.

Then, with a sound like ice cracking on the river on a winter's morning, came the rat-a-tat of knuckles on their garden gate. Hannah looked at her mother, eyes wide, as the sound of the gate's creaky hinge sounded. Whoever it was hadn't waited to be invited in.

What Hannah saw in her mother's eyes frightened her beyond anything else that day, even the drunk angry men, or Reverend Harte shaking her and screaming at her, or the burning effigy. What she saw in her mother's eyes was something she had never seen there before—fear.

In the gloom of the bush and tree branches that hid their garden gate from view, a tall figure pushed through. He still held his tricorn hat in his hand, probably to keep it from being knocked away as he ducked under the vines to get to them.

When he straightened, Hannah stared straight into the vat of bubbling fruit juice, terrified to meet his eyes. Reverend Harte had come after her, of course. Maybe he'd seen her running from the scene. And now he was standing feet from her, looking only slightly more composed than he had on the piers. He must have run at least as hard as she had.

"Reverend Harte!" Hannah heard her mother say in a smooth measured voice, nothing like what Hannah had seen in her eyes. "This *is* a surprise. What brings you here at such an hour?"

"Why don't you ask your daughter that, Mistress Cardozo?"

Hannah flinched from the seething anger just below the surface of those words, raising her eyes from the pot to meet the monster's gaze. He stood across the table, eyes boring into her. The knuckles on the hands holding his hat in front of him were white, gripping the edge of the hat so fiercely it looked like he might rip it in two.

Hannah opened her mouth to reply, feeling the bolus of truth start to bubble up under that imperious gaze, when her mother stepped between the two of them, breaking his line of vision.

"Hannah?" Rebekah asked, not even looking at her daughter. "Why would Hannah know anything about your doings, sir? Why, she has been here with me all afternoon and evening, making apple butter." Rebekah gestured at the table, where rows upon rows of small crockware pots stood, each covered with muslin and tied with twine. There must have been forty of them cooling on that table.

Reverend Harte did not say anything. He barely glanced at the jars. "But she wasn't, Mistress Cardozo. She was at the wharves. With my slave. Who is now missing." He spoke jerkily, blurting out each phrase and turning his bottled-fury gaze from mother to daughter. His eyes stuck on Hannah, who was mesmerized by the anger and violence she saw there. "Where did she go, Hannah? Where did you take Chastity?"

Hannah was torn. She was trained to be honest, especially to men of the cloth. But she had just heard her mother lie outright to this man, a man whom she knew to be cruel. "I don't know what you mean?" she said steadily.

"But you *do!*" Reverend Harte roared, slamming one palm onto the table and making both the crockware and the women jump. "You do! And you will tell me if it's the very last thing you do on this earthly plane." He started around the table toward Hannah, hands hooked into claws in front of him, moving with lethal quickness. Hannah squealed and held the dripping spoon up in front of her like a weapon.

Before he could reach her, Rebekah stepped again in front of him.

"Madam," he whispered, still staring at Hannah over her mother's shoulder. "I will only ask you once to move. I need to interrogate your daughter. You will not stand in my way."

"Yes, I will," Rebekah's voice rang out, drowning out the hiss and pop of the hearth behind them. "I most certainly *will*, sir."

Hannah flinched, but Rebekah didn't move.

"It is obvious to anyone who looks at her that this girl has been making apple butter for hours." Rebekah stepped slightly aside, enough for the Reverend to see Hannah but not enough for him to lunge by.

Reverend Harte took in the slash of preserve across Hannah's front, and when his eyes traveled up to her face, she willed herself not to flinch again.

"I have been making apple butter with my mother," she said, as clearly and calmly as she could manage. *I have been stirring this pot for the past minute, so maybe it's not a lie?*

Reverend Harte sneered, his face creasing into folds of anger and disgust. "You will regret this."

Rebekah shielded Hannah with her body, as if she could block her daughter from the man's hate.

"You'll see." The Reverend's voice began to rise almost as if he was preaching from the pulpit. "We'll run you out just like we ran out all the rest! If we can't run you off, we will beat it out of you or kill you. You'll never win, can't you see that? Never!"

He made as if to lunge past Rebekah again, to get at Hannah, but Rebekah wouldn't budge. She didn't make a move, but suddenly she looked bigger, more substantial. The Reverend stopped dead in his approach and looked at Rebekah with what might've been wonder.

Hannah had never loved anyone more in her entire life than she loved her mother in that moment.

"I don't think so, Reverend Harte," Rebekah said. "What do you think the townsfolk would say if they knew that you, the Reverend, were over here at this time of night, without an invitation, hurling insults and threats at a helpless woman and her young daughter? Doesn't seem very Christian to me."

The Reverend sucked in his breath with a sudden rattle and turned his sharp gaze to his surroundings, as if noticing them for the first time.

"Mistress Cohen over there," Rebekah went on, jerking her

head over her shoulder at their neighbor's house. "She doesn't sleep soundly, wakes up at the smallest of disturbances, you know. Our cat pads across her rooftop and she's wide awake."

Reverend Harte looked up at Mistress Cohen's window and, sure enough, a small blossom of wavering light came from within.

"Master Franco and his family as well," this time Rebekah jerked her chin at the dark house across the small garden lane. "That family has a lot of sons, most of them grown with families of their own. But not the last two. And they're the biggest of the lot."

The Reverend threw a glance at the Francos' house, and then turned back to Rebekah. She still hadn't moved. She stood, immovable as a boulder, between him and Hannah, hands on her hips. A silent stand-off ensued, with each party staring down the other. Hannah began to tremble uncontrollably. Almost imperceptibly, Hannah watched Rebekah's hand as it left her hip and reached behind to wrap around an iron poker leaning up against the base of the hearth, slowly picking it up and hiding it in the folds of her skirt.

"As I said, Reverend, we have a close community here. We look out for one another. And before anyone gets the wrong idea about what's going on here," Rebekah paused, letting this fully sink in, "I'd like to give you the opportunity to take your leave."

The Reverend still stood, leaning menacingly toward them as if he'd like to reach over Rebekah's shoulder and pluck Hannah up.

"Now," Rebekah said. She didn't yell, and she didn't need to.

The Reverend narrowed his eyes, taking in a quick, vicious breath through his flared nostrils and, in one quick motion, picked up one of the jars and hurled it at their back door. It struck the broad stone that served as the step with a thunk and didn't break, but the force of it knocked the muslin askew. Apple butter splashed all over their whitewashed door, staining it as if with blood. He jammed his hat angrily on his head and stalked back around the table in three long strides and out the back garden gate in four more. Then he was gone, only trembling branches left in his wake.

Incoherently, as she watched the brown viscous goo drip down onto their stone stoop, Hannah thought, *Blood of the Lamb*. The trembling came back, and Hannah sat down with a sudden thump. She still held the wooden spoon.

"I'm so sorry, Mama," she whispered. "I'm so sorry about all of this." Hot tears spilled down her cheeks. Rebekah squatted in front of her, took the wooden spoon out of her daughter's hand, and wiped the tears and apple butter off her face with her apron.

"Look at me," Rebekah put one finger under Hannah's chin, forcing it up. *"Look at me."*

Hannah looked into her mother's wide-set eyes only inches from her own.

"Listen and listen good. You did not create any of this; hate did. Only hate can cause this type of evil."

Hannah then fell into Rebekah, wrapping her arms around her mother's waist and sobbing. Rebekah sat down next to her and gathered her into her arms, smoothing the curls from her temples.

"I am proud of you, *gatinha*, so proud. You did what was right and fought the evil. And Bintu, did she escape?"

Hannah sniffled, thinking of Bintu's form ducking into the captain's quarters. She nodded against her mother's chest.

"What a wonder you are, my darling. You fought against evil and, today, you won."

Hannah cried even harder at the memory of the Reverend's leering face.

"But what if he comes back? What if he wants to question me again?" she asked between hitching sobs.

"If he comes back, we will not fear him, although he is something to be feared. If Bintu is well and away, he will have no proof. He can say whatever he'd like, but there's no proof."

When the sobbing storm had mostly passed and Hannah's breath was slowing, she finally got a good look at all the stoneware jars her mother had out on the table.

"Did you really make all this apple butter," she asked, "just to save me?"

Rebekah laughed, a sharp bark, and hugged her daughter harder, rocking them both. "Of course, my child. I would make twice as much apple butter to save you."

Despite it all, Hannah smiled.

CHAPTER 26

The next few days were misery to Hannah, and for no particular reason. They wouldn't hear from Uncle Aaron if Bintu was safe for months, and there was nothing she could do in the meantime.

The town was roiling with unrest. Since the mob had rolled through the streets and burned the effigy at the wharves, there had been another mob marching, except this one was made up of mostly slaves and, because of this, the march was not as well received as the one that was made up of mostly Whites. In fact, it was deemed downright dangerous by the landholders and slaveowners, so they quickly quashed it.

Her mother wasn't letting Hannah far out of her sight, and for good reason. They hadn't seen hide nor hair of Reverend Harte, but Rebekah had heard through the grapevine that the Hartes had lost a slave girl to a daring escape. There were whispers of it in the aisles of their store. Every time Hannah heard someone mention "escape" or "Hartes' girl," she tried to creep closer to whomever was talking, but somehow Rebekah would always intercept her and ward her off.

Hannah couldn't blame her mother. She was scared; they both were. Every night, Rebekah locked their doors and windows, keeping out the men who might hurt them.

Of course, even Hannah's most frightening imaginings of Reverend Harte or the thugs who attacked Harry at the school were nothing to what would actually happen to Bintu if she were caught out there. Every day they didn't hear anything about Bintu from the outside world was a good day in Hannah's book.

But Hannah was still here, and she felt more stuck than ever. She felt as if everyone had just up and left her and that, years from now, she would still be here, in the aisles of her mother's shop, measuring out flour and sugar and bolts of fabric into eternity.

That's why, the first chance she got to make a delivery, she jumped at it.

Ironically, it was to the same house that she'd delivered to that first time she'd seen Bintu up on the auction block. It felt like so many years ago.

Her mother was nervous, but there was nothing to be done about it. She needed the basket delivered, and Hannah was the only one on hand to do it. As Rebekah packed up the assortment of pantry staples into one of their large woven delivery baskets, she lectured Hannah about the dos and don'ts of her latest venture.

"Do not take the main roads, I mean none of them, not Broad or King or any of them. Do you hear, child?"

"Yes, Mama."

"And try to stick to the shadows, don't walk in full sunlight, and wear that bonnet tightly cinched." Rebekah turned the girl by her shoulders and fiddled with the ties of her bonnet. Hannah was taller than her mother now, something that had happened so quickly Hannah hadn't noticed.

"Hannah," Rebekah looked forlornly at her daughter.

"Mother." Hannah put her hands over her mother's. "I will be careful, stay in the shadows, and keep my head down."

"Promise?"

"I promise." Hannah gave her a quick hug, and then turned back to the basket, tucking a scrap of cloth over the top to protect the wares within. She felt like she needed to leave before her mother called her back. "I can take care of myself now, Mama. Promise."

With that she turned and headed out the front of the store, moving too quickly to hear her mother whisper under her breath, "I sincerely hope so, my child. I hope so."

Hannah knew she had promised, but she just had to know what had become of her boys. She thought she'd just pop back over, just to see if they were all right. She was so worried about them that she couldn't stay away. If she went to the school and saw nothing was amiss, she wouldn't go in. She just needed to make sure that they were all right.

She felt less sure of herself coming up the lane to the school. She started to feel off, her stomach queasy. She couldn't tell, as she approached, if all was as it should be. It looked as it always did—yellow painted clapboard with white trim, only peeling a little. She stopped at a distance.

What if Harry is angry because I returned? She'd promised him she'd stay away.

Hannah set the basket down on the side of the road and stood, undecided and biting her lip, looking at the school. She couldn't see any movement, and, odder still, she didn't see any smoke coming from the cook fire in the back garden. Perhaps Harry was having a cold supper, she reasoned, and didn't need the fire after the noonday meal with the boys. She wasn't convinced. Something about the scene looked off, and she couldn't quite tell what.

Hannah plunked herself down on the slight rise off to the side of the road until she could think of a way to approach. She didn't want to scare the boys or put them in danger. Around back would be the most straightforward way to get into the school. She could just hop the fence, cut through the garden she and Bintu had tended all summer, and enter through the back door.

She startled. *The garden!* She could go peek in at their garden without *actually* entering the property and see if it was tended, if her tree needed water, that sort of thing. The state of the garden would tell her about the state of things inside the school as well, she hoped.

Hannah stood, spotting a likely looking bush to push her basket under. It would be safe here for a while. There weren't many people about. Since the mobs, folks were going about their daily business, but with the fast gait and backward glances of the fearful.

Satisfied that her mother's wares would be untouched for the moment, Hannah turned her attention to the school. Her eyes gleamed green amidst all her freckles, and the breeze batted at the curly tendrils framing her face.

She started around the low-slung building to the right, ducking around the corner and following a stile fence bordered by an unkempt hedge stretching three quarters of the way down. The unruliness of the hedge wasn't itself a worry; it had always been that way. None of them ever found the time, between teaching and cooking and cleaning and tending the garden, to bother about the hedge. Besides, it gave them a modicum of protection from prying eyes. And for Harry and his school, there were plenty of prying eyes.

Hannah thought of Mistress Harte's sneering countenance as she'd stood in all her self-righteous glory in Harry's classroom. That was until Harry smacked the smile off of her face with his quick-witted replies. Hannah laughed, a quick wistful guffaw, at the memory of Harry taking Mistress Harte to town with his knowledge of the Scripture. Now that was class.

Her smile faded as the hedge petered out into a snarly butt-end of half-desiccated vines woven through the lower edge of the hedge. She could see into the back garden and their kitchen now. But the first thing she saw was her tree. Hannah's tree.

The tree was only a trifle more robust the day it had been planted than it was on this one. Even the scrap of calico that she'd tied around it in a sentimental gesture was now faded by the sun, the pattern barely discernible. The tree stood, a mere scrap of sticks with a calico collar, amongst a jumble of weeds and overgrown crops. The rue, Hannah saw as she approached the stile fence, had gone to flower, its itchy poison disguised in clusters of tiny, lemon-yellow blooms. The small plot of corn was dried up, husks dangling from each stalk like shingles hanging off an abandoned home.

Everything had gone to seed or flower. The whole garden had up and bloomed and no one had tended to it, because no one had been here to tend it. Cold fingers poked her stomach, clenching her insides in a fist.

No one is here. She could now see how obvious the signs were.

Not only was the tree almost completely dried up, and the garden a weedy mess, but their kitchen table and hearth were neglected as well. Worst of all, the cauldron with the little feet that they would use to boil water for cleaning, drinking, and the like had been tipped over and its contents long ago sloshed into the hearth itself, something that would never have happened on her or Bintu's watch. The coals had extinguished and congealed, now a dirty blackened mess like dried tar.

Each new sign of abandonment she saw made Hannah utter a little sigh or gasp of pain. It was horrible to see Harry's school in such a state. It made her want to cry, but she was almost too sad to cry. It was more than that, words like *heartbreak, sorrow, misery*, came to mind. Words she avoided teaching Bintu in their time together.

Her face, which a moment ago had been buoyant at the thought of Harry squaring off with Mistress Harte, now creased in pain, the lines of age stitched into her young face.

Hannah decided quickly that no one at the school would be bothered by her return because no one was there. She crossed the fence, rucking up her skirt and swinging her legs up and over the papery wooden stiles, one at a time. Mistress Harte would probably find her most unseemly, showing her petticoats to any Johnny-come-lately that might wander by, but Hannah didn't care a whit. She wasn't that far away from catching frogs and climbing the live oaks. She hopped down into the garden and the first thing she did was lope over to her abandoned hearth and right her cauldron. She couldn't stand seeing it tipped over like that. It just wouldn't do. Then she found an abandoned wooden bucket with some remnants of rainwater in it and poured it onto the base of her tree. It wasn't enough water, but it was some.

Hannah had never felt such a combination of emotions. Once she had finished pouring out the bucket, she dropped it and pressed a hand over her mouth, as if to muffle a scream, although she didn't make a sound.

She felt responsible for what had happened here, especially the neglect. She knew logically that it wasn't her fault. Harry had said in no uncertain terms that they would all be in danger if she stayed, but she still felt such utter shame. An untended end of the summer had browned out everything, leaving it a snarled mess.

When she turned her gaze to the school, it felt as if those dark windows were staring at her with a corpse's eyes. Accusing her. And then she saw it, in the corner of the window on the far right; one of the panes had broken, leaving a triangle of empty space. Hannah knew for a fact that Harry would not have stood for a broken window. *Too untidy. Never.*

It was the sight of this broken window that made the loss of Harry and his school feel like the sharp jagged end of a broken tooth in her heart. It jabbed, its crooked edges biting and sharp, but she couldn't stop returning to it.

What happened? Where's Harry? Hannah had an awful feeling that she would never find out. She lowered her head and wept into the dusty folds of her skirt.

After a while, she began to feel like herself again and wiped the tears from her face. She thought she'd been there all afternoon, but according to the sun, it had only been about half an hour. She should be getting back. She'd have to double-time her grocery delivery to avoid her mother's suspicion. She stood, dusted off her skirts, and swiped once more at her eyes.

When she turned to the school in the ruins of her garden, she found herself walking up to the back door and putting a hand on the latch. She hadn't planned on going in, but she thought she'd peek. Only a few minutes look around and then she'd be off. Maybe she'd find some clue as to what had happened.

She pushed open the heavy door at the back of the classroom, not surprised it wasn't locked. Harry rarely locked it, and she couldn't imagine he'd think to do it under duress.

The door creaked inwards, revealing an unused dusty space. The light from the clouded windows fell through floating debris like layered cumulus clouds. The details of the outside world were hazy through the yellow scrim on the windowpanes. The scarred wooden table was abandoned in the middle of the room and had a layer of dust on it. Hannah put her finger in it and swiped, leaving a long stripe behind.

The room had the hot close feel of a place that had been shut up for too long. As she looked around, she could almost hear the ghost of the boys laughing, and the stern, solemn cadence of Harry's recitations. She spun slowly in a circle, savoring the memories.

Thinking of Harry made her wince, and she decided to head up to his quarters to see if he had left some sign or note there, indicating where he'd gone. She started toward the narrow stairs at the back and, just as she put her hand on the rope rail that led up into the hot musty attic rooms, a shadow fell across her face.

She whirled, her heart suddenly in her throat, fluttering like a trapped bird. *Is someone here? Reverend Harte? What if he followed me here?*

The shadow passed across another window. Whoever was out there wasn't trying to hide, and they were making right for the open back door Hannah had just come through. A cold sweat beaded her brow as she looked from the stairs to the back door and to the stairs again.

Should I run? Head upstairs? If he'd already seen her, she'd be trapped if she went to the attic.

Then another thought passed through her mind. *What if it's one of those two bloodthirsty maniacs they sent to get Harry the first time?* She began to shake all over, her feet still frozen to the spot. The shadow started to creep across the final window. It stopped halfway, testing the air or listening.

As quietly as she could, she began to back slowly up the stairs, her eyes glued to what she could see of the outside. She crept up one step, then the next, and then the next, inching her way up and out of sight. Any moment, he would lunge at her through the window, or race around back and through the door. She kept expecting to see the dark cloth of his cape, but it never came.

What finally slipped into view was the assassin cat, King Sol, huge lantern eyes gazing inquisitively as his tail flickered this way and that.

Hannah belted out her pent-up breath in a gush of laughter and relief.

"You! You gave me such a fright!"

He yawned. She laughed again at her own folly and sat heavily onto the middle riser of the stairs, which shifted with the sudden addition of her weight. Her bottom slipped toward the back and the board she was sitting on canted ever so slightly to the front.

Surprised, she looked down and saw a dark triangular crack running along the back of the stair, where the step and the riser met.

A hiding place. Harry has a hiding place.

Squatting on the stair below, she yanked on the stubborn riser, urging it out of its close join. After a couple of tugs, it came loose, almost throwing her backward. She propped the step up against the wall of the narrow stairway and, after just a moment's hesitation, stuck her hand into the darkness under the stairs, pawing around to see if anything was there. Her knuckles clunked into the corner of something, and she lifted it up. It was heavy and angular and, when she brought it out into the musty light, she recognized it instantly.

It was Harry's Bible, the one he'd learned to read with, and eventually taught himself to write with, and from which he'd taught hundreds of children how to read, and how to teach their families to read. Whatever had happened, Harry had found the time to hide his Bible.

Hannah turned around and sat on the step below the hidey hole. She raised the Bible to her lips and blew, sending dust swirling into the stairway.

She looked up to thank King Sol for startling her into this revelation, but her feline friend was gone without a trace, perhaps gone off in search of Bintu.

The dark red ribbon Harry used as a place-marker was sticking out the bottom of the Bible. Hannah opened it, carefully turning the thin pages until she'd reached Harry's spot. She was not surprised to see that he had put the place marker in Exodus, but she was surprised to find another slip of paper there, one with her name on it.

She picked it out of the pages and looked at Harry's lovely looping scrawl of her name. She smiled, remembering when he taught her the word *palindrome* specifically because her name was one—same going forward as it was going back. *What did he say?*

"It's important to know the power of your name, Hannah. There is so much power in our names. Yours, for instance, means grace or mercy. Did you know that?"

Hannah hadn't known that, but he had taught her.

She unfolded the small slip of paper.

Dear Hannah,

Never forget what you learned in this school. I shall never forget you.

~Harry

Hannah scanned the Bible page and was amazed when her eyes fell upon a verse. It was the Song of Miriam, the very same verse she'd been talking about to Bintu the day they'd said goodbye.

Then Miriam the prophet, Aaron's sister, took a timbrel in her hand, and all the women followed her, with timbrels and dancing. Miriam sang to them:

Sing to the Lord,

for he is highly exalted.

Both horse and driver

he has hurled into the sea.

Hannah sat for a long time on the step, staring at the verses until the words began to swim. Then she carefully tucked the note back into the Bible, stood, and replaced the step where it was. She looked around for what she knew was her last glimpse of the schoolroom, and then she left to finish her mother's delivery, toting the Bible with her.

CHAPTER 27
Charleston 1831

On a drizzly evening in late January, my granddaughter put her hand on my knee, jolting me out of my memories. The past rushed away from me as the present poured back in like a waterfall.

"Nonna?" Rachel asked, looking into my face with her young one, so much like my own at that age.

"Yes, hummingbird?" The cobwebs of memory still hung heavily around me. I tried to shake them off, but Bintu and Harry and Charles Town and that terrible, wonderful summer wouldn't leave so readily.

"Do you still have it?"

"What's that?"

"His Bible? Harry's Bible."

I brushed my brow as if to sweep the last heady strands of that long-lost story away. "Of course I do. I kept it, throughout everything that came after." I rose from my seat, noting that the hearth had burned down considerably. I must have been spinning my tale for a long time. "Let me see," I mused as I hobbled toward my bookcase, stopping only to toss another birch log onto the fire. It was almost sunset, judging by the opaque grey beyond the windowpanes, and it would soon be the Sabbath.

I stopped in front of my meager bookcase. Some books had come and gone, but I had always held onto Harry's. Through the unrest of the colonies becoming independent of the Crown, and everything that came after that—the Revolution, the uniting of the colonies into the United States of America, and my own personal fight for the end of slavery—I had always held on to Harry's Bible as if it were a life raft. In fact, all I had done, the Hebrew Orphan Society, all the work for freedom of education, had been for them—for Harry, for Bintu, and for myself, as well as for Rachel and the generations to come. That Bible was a spark in the dark, a lighthouse beam pulsing with even, steady hope.

I braced my lower back with my hands and creakily stretched, scanning the spines until I found the large tome I was looking for. The spine crumbled a little under my grasp as I pulled it away from the shelf and I smoothed my palm over its aged surface. The memories were still close, stirring just under the surface.

I brought it over to my Rachel and plopped it carefully into her waiting hands.

"Careful with the pages, hummingbird, they are so very thin."

She nodded, wide-eyed, and opened the cover with care, leafing through the translucent yellow pages.

Lantern light outside the window caught my attention. Someone was coming up the path. It wasn't quite dark, but it would be in a quarter of an hour. The family had arrived. Rachel and I only had a few more moments of our own together.

I took up the challah bread and placed it in the center of the table with a saucer of salt, just as my mother used to. The oil came next and then the tapers, my final act for the evening. An idea occurred to me as I touched the flame to the maiden wick of the last candle.

"Rachel," I asked, not looking at her but gazing critically at the laid table. It looked beautiful, the silver gleaming in the candlelight and the warm, shiny skin of the braided challah giving off a toasty aroma.

"Hmmm?" she answered, still distracted by the book in her lap. She was being *very* careful. That was my girl.

"Remember how I told you about that tree my boys planted for me? In the school garden?"

"Yes, I do. A peach tree, wasn't it?"

"That's right. Would you like to go see it tomorrow? With me? It's still there. Although the school is now part of the parsonage, they kept the garden and back kitchen largely how we had it when it was Harry's school."

Rachel looked up, eyes shining. "Oh yes, Nonna, I would love that. Harry was my favorite of all the parts of your story."

Two more blurs of light were making their way up the front path.

"Harry was wonderful," I murmured. "He was really, really wonderful."

A light knock came at the front door.

The next morning, Rachel was ready, bright-eyed and bushy-tailed, for our adventure. We both wore heavy cloaks and, when we stepped outside, our breath steamed in the air and the sunlight glanced off the trees like diamond shards. I closed the door behind me and latched it. Rachel had already set off, skipping from flagstone to flagstone.

"Rachel," I called after her. "A moment." She obediently returned to my side, and I pulled a gingham scrap of fabric out of my pocket, turned her briskly around, gathered her unruly curls in my fist, and wrapped the cloth around the bun.

"There," I said. "Ready for our journey." I took her hand and led her down the path.

We walked in silence, Rachel's small hand nestled in my own like a warm, fledgling bird. I could tell she was pondering something, turning it over in her quick mind. When she addressed me, I was waiting for her question.

"Nonna? What happened to them? To Bintu? And to Harry?"

Even though I had guessed the direction her questions would take, it still hurt my heart to answer. "I don't know what happened to them. We never heard what had happened to Harry. There were rumors, but they weren't very nice."

"And Bintu?"

I paused, and looked down into her bright upturned face, surprised to see the sparkle of tears in her eyes.

"Well," I said. "Uncle Aaron told me he had seen her safely off of the ship, but after that?" I shrugged.

Rachel nodded and looked down at her feet.

"But years later, I found a package on my doorstep, and I believe it was from Bintu."

"What was in it?"

"Treasure."

Rachel gasped and her hand went immediately to the necklace at her throat. "This treasure?" she asked in a small, breathy voice.

"The very same." I smiled and put my hand on Rachel's shoulder for support. "The very same." We started off again at a slow pace.

In half an hour, we had reached the site of Harry's old school. Now a part of the parsonage and someone's home, a small trickle of smoke bled into the sky from the chimney.

We wound around to the back garden, and I was pleasantly surprised to see that whoever lived there was using the same layout that Bintu and I had, so many years ago. And the peach tree was huge despite the neglect it had faced its first summer. It had grown to mammoth proportions in the interim and branched out over the hedge and fence.

"Hello, old friend," I said, reaching up and tugging one of the branches. "Come here, Rachel," I called over my shoulder.

Rachel had been looking over the fence at the winter garden, all sticks and frozen stones. I imagined her picturing the people I had told her about who were now lost to the tides of time. For a moment, they became real again, superimposed over the frost-blasted hummocks of ground. It felt like, just for a moment, they had become real, and I was the ghost.

Rachel skipped up, looking at me expectantly. I tugged the scrap of gingham and freed her curls, which sprang from her head in a joyous corona.

I reached both hands up and creakily tied the cloth onto one of the spindly branches of the peach tree, its joints as knotted as my own. As I slowly tied the scrap around a branch, the line from the paper Rachel had found floated back to me, "*Tzedek Tzedek Tirdof.* Justice, justice shall you pursue, that you may live."

I released the branch from my grasp and it sprang away, free, waving the gingham scrap proudly in the air, like a banner. For a moment, I stood looking at the school that had taught me so much, and I could almost see her dark figure moving at work behind the scarred table by the hearth. I could almost feel the intensity of that light blue gaze. "That you may live, Bintu. Justice, that you may live."

I took my granddaughter by the hand and turned away from the past. Rachel looked back as we drew away and the necklace glinted at her throat, a silver hand dangling from a leather cord, Bintu's hand of protection.

ACKNOWLEDGMENTS

N o book worth its salt is written in isolation, and especially not this one.

We have many people to thank for their help, solid council, and expertise. We would especially like to thank our loosely constructed and dedicated advisory board. Rabbi Ira Schiffer, for his careful edits, help with the complexities of Hebrew, and his wise advice. Sally Z. Hare, distinguished professor emerita at Coastal Carolina University, for her generous time and effort to "get it perfect," down to the last detail. P. J. McGhee was an inestimable help with her keen eye to detail and tone.

We would also like to thank Randi Serrins and Anita Rosenberg from temple, Kahal Kadosh Beth Elohim for their time and effort to tour the temple and the cemetery and their expertise on the early history of the Jewish settlement in Charleston. The book would not have been as well researched without the encouragement of Nic Butler and the astounding help of the staff at the Charleston Public Library. Many thanks to them.

A note of huge thanks to Koehler books and their team for putting this whole thing together and see the light of day.

Finally, we owe an ongoing debt of gratitude to Jonas and Dyer who have to live with us while we write and trudge around cities and scour dusty archives.

CPSIA information can be obtained
at www.ICGtesting.com
Printed in the USA
LVHW031543280722
724574LV00004B/343

9 781646 635955